SECRETS OF THE JEDI

JEDI APPRENTICE

#1 The Rising Force
#2 The Dark Rival
#3 The Hidden Past
#4 The Mark of the Crown
#5 The Defenders of the Dead
#6 The Uncertain Path
#7 The Captive Temple
#8 The Day of Reckoning
#9 The Fight for Truth
#10 The Shattered Peace
#11 The Deadly Hunter
#12 The Evil Experiment
#13 The Dangerous Rescue
#14 The Ties That Bind
#15 The Death of Hope
#16 The Call to Vengeance
#17 The Only Witness
#18 The Threat Within

JEDI QUEST

#1 The Way of the Apprentice
#2 The Trail of the Jedi
#3 The Dangerous Games
#4 The Master of Disguise
#5 The School of Fear
#6 The Shadow Trap
#7 The Moment of Truth
#8 The Changing of the Guard
#9 The False Peace
#10 The Final Showdown

SECRETS OF THE JEDI

JUDE WATSON

SCHOLASTIC INC.

New York   Toronto   London   Auckland   Sydney
Mexico City   New Delhi   Hong Kong   Buenos Aires

www.starwars.com
www.scholastic.com

ISBN 0-439-53667-7

12 11 10 9 8 7 6 5 4   6 7 8 9 10/0

Printed in the U.S.A.
First printing, March 2005

Qui-Gon Jinn couldn't sleep. Every night he spent some time trying, but in the end he decided to walk off the need for rest.

He didn't understand it. As a Jedi, he was used to sleeping anywhere, in all sorts of conditions. He had slept in cargo holds and spaceport hangars and on a pile of droid parts. He had slept four hours in the middle of a field during a driving rainstorm. When he needed sleep, he told his mind to empty and his body to unwind, and they obeyed.

But in the past, he'd never had to deal with his heart.

He had done the forbidden. He had fallen in love with another Jedi Knight. He had pledged himself to her. And she had died. He was paying a price he was glad to pay, because those few days of loving and of knowing he was loved were worth it. But how to put his heart back together? Tahl had changed him. She had made him whole, and she had broken him with her death. Qui-Gon could not figure out how to reassemble.

So he didn't sleep. He and his Padawan, Obi-Wan

Kenobi, had been at the Jedi Temple for weeks now. Yoda had called them back for what they'd expected to be a briefing for a mission, but there had been no mission. "Need your Padawan does days of reflection," Yoda had said. "Important they are as days of action."

There had been much action lately. Mission after mission. The Senate was fractured, torn apart by special interests, by warring clans and alliances.

There seemed to be plenty Qui-Gon and Obi-Wan could be doing, but Qui-Gon did not want to cross Yoda, so they stayed. But the weeks at the Temple only made Qui-Gon's sleeplessness worse. He walked the empty halls at night. The glow lamps were powered down to a soft blue, making it a restful time to stroll. It seemed that every hall, every room, held a memory of Tahl, but he didn't court those memories. He tried to allow his grief to be his companion, not his master. He opened his mind and simply walked.

He found himself, at the end of a long night, back near his quarters. Qui-Gon hesitated. He was not ready to return to his small room and stare at the walls.

"Glad I am to find you awake." Yoda scuttled forward, leaning on his gimer stick.

He blinked at Qui-Gon. "And why, my friend, does sleep not find you?"

Qui-Gon did not want to discuss his heart with Yoda. He loved the Jedi Master, but he did not want to confide in him. He had never told Yoda of his feelings for Tahl, and there was no need for Yoda to know how close Qui-Gon had come to violating the rules of the Jedi Order. So instead of the full truth, he said, "I find peace from walking."

"See I do many things in you," Yoda said. "Peace is not one of them."

Qui-Gon didn't answer. He didn't shrug, or turn away, or drop his eyes. He knew Yoda would read the unspoken message. *I am not ready to talk about this.*

"Need a mission now, you do," Yoda said.

Qui-Gon nodded. "And you have one for me. It's about time."

Behind him he heard soft footsteps. The smell of rich tea came to his nostrils — his favorite, a blend from the leaves of a *sapir* plant, green and fragrant.

It must be near dawn, then. Obi-Wan had taken to brewing him tea and bringing it to his quarters in the early morning. Qui-Gon had gently tried to discourage him; he didn't want his Padawan to wait on him. But Obi-Wan, in his own stubborn way, kept showing up. Qui-Gon was both irritated and touched by this. Obi-Wan didn't know the details. But he was eighteen now, old enough to make a good guess as to what had happened on Apsolon between his Master and Tahl. He could sense the depths of Qui-Gon's sorrow, and he felt he had to do something to help, no matter how small.

Qui-Gon could feel him hesitating now, back behind a pillar. He did not want to interrupt his Master's conversation with Yoda.

"Step forward you may, Obi-Wan," Yoda said. "Concerns you, this does."

Obi-Wan came out of the shadows. Yoda took in everything in a glance — the small teapot on the tray, the steaming mug, the expression of concern in Obi-Wan's eyes.

His gaze returned to Qui-Gon. In that gaze Qui-Gon read the truth. Yoda knew of his nighttime walks. Yoda knew of the tea Obi-Wan brought every morning. And perhaps he even knew about Tahl. How could Qui-Gon have forgotten that there was so little that Yoda did not know?

Yoda had not called them back in order to give Obi-Wan a chance to reflect. He had called them back for Qui-Gon's sake.

"Not ready I am to let you go," Yoda said. "Yet let you go, I must."

CHAPTER 2

It all started with a young boy who liked to build things.

Talesan Fry was ten years old. He had long ago become bored with school. He much preferred to be home, in his room, working with devices he had built himself. At the age of eight, he had set up a communication system in his home that used voice activation to track his movements. At the age of nine, he had discovered how to get around it by giving the system a false reading so that his mother was never exactly sure where he was or what he was doing. Now, at the age of ten, he had moved on to spying on his neighbors. Perhaps it was a normal pursuit for a young boy, but in this case, Taly made a special effort to spy on neighbors who went to great lengths not to be overheard.

Breaking into the main comm channels on his home-world of Cirrus was too easy. What Taly liked to do was lurk. He would break into the secure channels, past the security gates, opening one after the other with a few tweaks and clicks on his system. He never heard anything very interesting. Politicians. Security officers. Corporate vice presidents. Nobody with anything worth saying, in his opinion. Still, he kept lurking, because he liked to do what was forbidden.

And then one day he heard something interesting. At first, it wasn't enough to even raise his head from the sleep couch, where he was listlessly flying a model of a Gion speeder by remote. He heard a quick exchange, a communication about a job coming up.

"Negative," someone said. "Concussive missiles attract too much attention in close quarters."

"Wouldn't hurt to have them. I don't care what our employer says. He's not doing the job, we are. No blood on his hands. I want to be able to blast my way out if I have to."

Slowly, Taly raised his head.

"If it comes to that, you'll have half the galactic security force on your tail. It's got to be in and out, quiet and quick."

"You think bagging the leader of —"

"No names." The voice was curt. Taly now had his ear against the transmitter. He had activated a recording rod.

His eyes widened as he listened. He could pick out five distinct voices and it didn't take him long to realize they were bounty hunters. Five bounty hunters working together? Taly didn't know much about bounty hunters, but he knew enough to be sure an alliance was highly unusual.

He knew he had stumbled onto something big. They were talking about a rendezvous on some planet, about an assassination. They had already picked the date, and it was only fourteen standard days away. This was something he could not keep to himself. Something — and this was worst of all — he would have to tell his parents about.

An hour later, after he'd worked up the courage, he brought them the recording rod. His parents were too alarmed to punish him. They contacted Cirrus security, who notified galactic security on Coruscant. Eventually the story of a boy who had information on a major assassination plot made its way to the Senate Investigating Commission on Crime Syndication, Dissemination, and Proliferation in the Core and Mid-Rim Systems. The commission had been deadlocked for two months on the question of whether the scope of their investigation should include the Outer Rim. Taly's news hit them like an electrojabber, prodding them into an action they had been reluctant to take. They called on him to be their star witness.

By the time this request had made it back to the Fry family on Cirrus, news of Taly's recording had reached enough security officials, Senators, and Senatorial aides that it might as well have been broadcast on the HoloNet. It didn't take long after that for a corrupt official to find the right person eager to bribe. Within two days, Talesan Fry was marked for death by the very bounty hunters he had overheard.

Taly's parents knew enough to realize that their boy had landed in the middle of a great deal of trouble. They decided to keep the recording rod and bring it themselves to Coruscant. They would let Taly testify in secret, and that would be the end of it.

The night before they were to leave, they were attacked at midnight. The raid failed only because of the attacker's arrogance. The bounty hunters did not pause to consider that a young boy capable of infiltrating their secure communications system would also be capable of fashioning a security system in his own home that could confound them.

Taly and his parents escaped in an airspeeder that took off from their roof as the lights and alarms sounded. The bounty hunter, working alone because the five had decided that only one was needed, found the recording device. He used a concussion missile to destroy the house. He used double the firepower he needed. He was annoyed.

Now Taly and his parents were in hiding, afraid to move, afraid to trust. The Senate commission realized they had bungled this job and asked the Jedi for help. In a galaxy where no one trusted anyone, most still trusted the Jedi. Taly's parents would allow them to escort the family to Coruscant.

The planet Cirrus was known for its golden seas and its lovely cities. The Jedi landed at the spaceport of the capital city of Ciran. The city folded around a vast bay that served to bounce the light, turning the sky pale yellow. Two orange suns blazed overhead. The combination of the golden light and the bright suns had a stunning effect, as though the very air was too bright to see.

Humans were native to Cirrus, but the streets were

thronged with many species. The city was built on two levels, with businesses below and residences above. Lift tubes and ramps were stationed at regular intervals. Ciran was a city that tried to control its air traffic by making walking pleasant and easy for its citizens. Large awnings — pieces of strong, flexible fabric — stretched across the walkways, providing shade and eliminating some of the glare. They rippled like colorful flags and cast shadows like rainbows.

"We must take care that we aren't followed," Qui-Gon said as they took the tube down from the spaceport to the business level. "The bounty hunters will no doubt expect the Senate to send some sort of security to pick up Talesan. They'll be watching, hoping we lead them to the Frys."

"I don't pick up anything," Adi Gallia said. "Siri?"

Obi-Wan hadn't seen Siri Tachi with her Master in years. He noted a new sense of respect when Adi turned to her Padawan. For the first time since they'd boarded the ship together at the Temple, Obi-Wan really looked at his friend. Siri was taller, certainly, but she also carried herself differently. There was less aggression in her stance. She had grown comfortable with herself. Her own beauty had once thoroughly annoyed Siri, but now Obi-Wan saw that she was more comfortable with it. She did not try as hard to hide it; she simply didn't care.

Siri hesitated before answering, as if she wanted to be sure. "Nothing."

"Good. Siri has an extraordinary sensitivity to Force

warnings," Adi told Qui-Gon. "She's gotten us out of quite a few tight spots."

"Well, I might sense the danger, but Adi gets us out of it," Siri amended, flashing her Master a grin.

"Just to be sure, let's walk a bit before we head for the Frys," Qui-Gon said.

Taly and his parents had kept moving since their home had been destroyed. They had chosen to hide in the densely populated city, moving from hotel to hotel, from hired room to hired room, not wanting to put friends in danger. The Jedi had received the coordinates of their current hide-out just as they landed. The Frys were expecting them.

They had taken refuge in an inn that catered to short-term residents, beings who traveled to Cirrus frequently on business. The inn did not advertise and was known only among the network of business travelers. It had no sign outside, just an anonymous door. Taly's father had known about it through his contacts.

The Jedi waited in an alley a few steps away, just to make certain they were not followed. When they were sure, they went to the door and pressed the button alongside a security monitor.

"Key in your code number," a voice from the monitor requested.

"We don't have one," Qui-Gon said. "We're looking —"

"Full up." The monitor blinked off.

Qui-Gon pressed the button again. "We are expected

by one of your guests," he said quickly, trying not to sound annoyed.

"Name?"

"Yanto." It was the name the Fry family was hiding under.

"One moment."

It was more than a moment, but the door slid open. The Jedi slipped inside. A heavy gray curtain was immediately in front of them. They pushed it aside and found themselves in a small circular hall. A round desk sat in the center of the space. The young man sitting behind it wore an expression of great boredom. He had long fair hair that he wore loose over his shoulders.

"They aren't in," he said. "I checked."

"We'd like to wait in their room," Qui-Gon said.

The young man shrugged.

Adi spoke crisply. "They left word that we could enter, didn't they?"

The clerk looked down at his datascreen. "I guess so."

"Then let us up." Adi's voice rang with authority.

The young man pushed a key card across the table. "Suite 2344. Have a ball."

The Jedi stepped into the turbolift. It rose swiftly to the top floor. They found the room. Qui-Gon knocked, and when there was no answer, he inserted the key card. A series of numbers flashed, and the door slid open.

The room was modest. Two sleep couches were in an

alcove, and a desk stood against a wall. Vidscreens and datascreens were recessed in the wall. One window over-looked the street but was covered by a gray curtain.

Siri checked out the travel bags near the sleep couches. "Looks like it could be them," she said. "Basic necessities are still here."

"So we wait," Adi said.

Qui-Gon went to the window and slid the curtain back a slight bit. He looked out onto the street. Obi-Wan watched his face.

"He let us up too easily," Qui-Gon said.

"We were expected," Adi said.

"He didn't ask our names."

"He didn't seem to care much about security," Obi-Wan said.

"Yes, he seemed to advertise his indifference," Qui-Gon murmured, his eyes darting around the room.

Siri bent over to examine the items more closely. She fingered a few items thrown on the end of the sleep couch. Suddenly, she straightened.

"Something's wrong," she said.

Qui-Gon turned, his gaze sharp. "Tell us."

"They aren't coming back." Siri indicated the items at her feet. "I sense it. These items are camouflage. There should be something personal here, and there isn't."

"Their house was destroyed," Adi said. "They might not have any personal items left." She said this not as a challenge, but as an observation, trying to focus Siri's thinking.

"That could be true," Siri said. "But still. They have been here for three days, they said. There should be evidence that they have been living here. A crumb of food. A loose thread. A stain on the clothes. A wrinkle. A scent. Something."

"And the clerk . . ." Qui-Gon said, but he didn't finish his thought.

"If they felt they had been traced here . . ." Siri said.

Obi-Wan looked at the others. He had felt nothing, no surge of the dark side. He had only felt the normal uneasiness of being in a strange place, knowing that who they were looking for was being hunted. He felt a flash of envy of Siri, who seemed tuned into Qui-Gon's thoughts.

Just then, Siri looked up. Her hand flew to her lightsaber hilt.

Qui-Gon was already moving, streaking to one side of the door. "The clerk. He's coming," he said, just as the door slid open and blaster fire pinged through the air.

CHAPTER 3

The being who burst through the door bore little resemblance to the bored clerk. Now he wore black armorweave body armor. A holster for a blaster rifle and vibroblade crisscrossed his back, and wrist rockets were strapped to his forearms. His long fair hair streamed behind him as he rolled into the room like a droideka, surprising the Jedi by the unusual angle of attack.

He rolled a Merr-Sonn fragmentation grenade into the center of the room. It exploded immediately, sending shrapnel in all directions. He rolled to a stop, crouching behind a lightweight shield.

Qui-Gon felt the air shimmer with the blast, and the shrapnel exploded around him. He leaped in front of Obi-Wan and Siri to protect them. It was hard for even a Jedi Master to deflect grenade shrapnel. It was fast, unpredictable, random. It took all of Qui-Gon and Adi's concentration to block it. The shrapnel was flung back from their lightsabers and slammed into the walls and floors. A few deadly missiles thudded into the bounty hunter's shield, but they bounced off.

Qui-Gon saw the flash of surprise on the bounty hunter's face at the sight of lightsabers. No doubt he'd been expecting a standard Senate security force, not a Jedi team. He fired off two wrist rockets in rapid succession, then backtracked, rolling out through the door again.

On his exit, he tossed another grenade inside the room. Qui-Gon leaped forward and turned it into a hunk of smoking metal before it exploded. He kept his eyes on the bounty hunter. He had paused for an instant outside the door. A flash of something lit the bounty hunter's eyes, and he turned around and fled.

Qui-Gon raced out as the bounty hunter blasted a hole through the hall window with his wrist rocket, then flew through the shattered panes. Qui-Gon saw a liquid cable line arc out.

He reached the window and looked down. He could just see the silver cable slithering back down through the air. The bounty hunter had landed on the pedestrian walkway below. Within seconds he had been swallowed up by the crowd, disappearing underneath one of the colorful awnings.

Adi stood next to him. "He was waiting for them. Figured he would take us out in the meantime."

"At least we know one thing," Obi-Wan said. "He doesn't know where they are."

"I'm not so sure about that," Qui-Gon murmured.

He strode back to the hallway outside the blasted door.

He stood where the clerk had stood. A flash of surprise had lit his eyes, a revelation, and then smugness and purpose. All of this Qui-Gon had seen.

The bounty hunter, once disguised as the clerk, knew where they had gone.

There was so little time. The bounty hunter was already on his way. But Qui-Gon didn't let himself think of that. He slowly considered each object he could see from this vantage point.

Floor. Corner of a window. Corner of vidscreen. A pillow on the sleep couch. The edge of a pack.

Nothing.

Qui-Gon looked at the door itself. Then the keypad that they'd used to enter.

"The keycode," he said. "I know hotels like this. The occupant chooses a code that is easy to remember. The code is entered into security and on the individual cards. The occupant can either use the card or key in the number to get inside the room."

Adi nodded.

Qui-Gon lifted a hand, and the door card flew from where he'd left it on the sill and into his hand. He swiped the card and noted the number sequence that flashed.

"The code here is 2N533," Qui-Gon said. "The city of Ciran is shaped like a five-pointed star. There are five districts, and coordinates and addresses reflect that. Every address starts with the district number. 'N' could mean north."

"You think the key code is the address where they are staying?" Adi asked.

"That's taking a chance," Siri said. "Wouldn't they be afraid the bounty hunter would figure it out?"

"They didn't know he was here. They just knew he was close. But they had to leave us a hint."

"Besides," Obi-Wan said, "he wasn't sure they were gone for good. He was waiting for them to return."

As he spoke, he was already accessing the map of Ciran on his datapad. "2N533," he said. "Without a street name, I'll have to cross-check . . . wait . . ." He looked up. "District 2, 533 North Ascin Street. That's the only 533 address that's in the second district and has a north designation. It's got to be it."

"The bounty hunter has a head start," Adi said. "We can't afford to make a mistake."

"He is on foot," Qui-Gon said. "So are we. So we must be faster."

CHAPTER 4

They ran through the streets, never hesitating, never stopping. Their Jedi training helped them. Obi-Wan was able to memorize the map in seconds. Siri was able to point out shortcuts. Qui-Gon and Adi used the Force to find the easiest way through the crowd.

They saw no sign of the bounty hunter. When they got to the address, Qui-Gon and Adi stopped to study the façade. It was a building of gray stone, appearing identical to the other residences surrounding it.

Qui-Gon crossed the street and stood in front of the door. He raised his hand to push the indicator bell on the intercom.

He felt it before it came. A window flipped open overhead and a large vibroblade swung down. He felt the whistle of the wind against his back as he jumped. Another second and it would have gone through his head.

Obi-Wan sprang forward to help his Master, and Adi and Siri began to move around him, trying to see in the windows by the door.

"There appear to be" — Adi started as darts flew out of a concealed panel — "booby traps."

"Enough of this," Qui-Gon muttered. "There isn't time."

He unsheathed his lightsaber and cut a hole in the door.

An oily, slick substance rolled out and covered the floor, splashing on Qui-Gon. He looked down at his soiled boots.

Blaster fire suddenly pinged from the lift tube. Qui-Gon swung his lightsaber to deflect it, not moving an inch.

"We're Jedi!" he thundered. "Stop this! There's no time!"

The blaster fire stopped.

The door of the lift tube was cracked slightly, the seam open just enough to give someone hiding a narrow view into the room. It opened a few more centimeters.

A boy poked his head out. His hair was red and stuck up in tufts all over his head. His eyes were a vivid green. His narrow, pointed nose twitched. Next to him were a man and woman. They each held blasters, but slowly lowered them as they saw Qui-Gon's lightsaber.

"We didn't know," the woman said.

Qui-Gon sheathed his lightsaber. "We understand."

"I am Nelia Fry. This is my husband, Grove. And this is Taly."

The boy pointed to the floor. "If you move, you'll slip. That's synthetic oil mixed with soap. My own recipe."

"I won't slip," Qui-Gon said, just as he took a step and slipped sideways. He regained his balance, slipped again, and slid into the lift tube door. His hands slapped against it and his aggrieved face was now centimeters from Talesan's.

"Sorry?" Taly offered.

Adi Force-leaped over the slippery mess and landed next to Qui-Gon. "We have to leave immediately. A bounty hunter is on your trail. He has this address."

The family exchanged worried glances. "No matter where we go, he finds us," Grove Fry said.

"We have an exit plan," Nelia said. "We have swoop bikes on the roof."

The Jedi hurried the family aboard the lift tube and it took them swiftly up to the roof.

There were three swoops, fully fueled. "We'll have to double up," Qui-Gon said. "Talesan, ride with me."

"Call me Taly," the boy said. "I have a feeling we're going to hang around together for awhile."

"If you two can fit on this swoop, my Padawan can take the pilot seat," Qui-Gon told Nelia and Grove. "We left our ship near the landing platform, in a secure location."

Just then a transmitter on Grove's belt blinked rapidly. "Someone else has entered the building," he said worriedly. "Taly rigged up a silent alarm."

"He's here," Siri said quietly.

"It's going to take him a few minutes to search," Qui-Gon said. "Let's go."

Grove and Nelia exchanged a glance. "We're not coming with you."

"What do you mean?" Qui-Gon asked.

"Dad? Mom?" Taly's voice suddenly sounded very young.

Nelia crouched to look into her son's eyes. "Dad and I think you'll be safer without us. He is too close. If we wait and leave a few seconds after you, he might follow us instead. We can lead him away from you. Give you time to get far from here."

"This isn't necessary," Adi said crisply. "We can protect you."

"We mean no disrespect," Grove said. "We trust the Jedi. But we also want every chance for our son."

"You must come with us," Qui-Gon argued. "To stay is too great a risk."

Grove's eyes filled with steely determination.

"That is for us to decide, not you," he said. "We have talked about this at length; we know what we have to do. Nothing you can say will convince us. And you cannot force us. If we can do any small thing to save our son, we will. You have a better chance without us, especially if we create a distraction. That is our decision."

"We'll find our way to Coruscant," Nelia told Taly. "We'll find you."

Taly had gone very still.

Nelia straightened quickly. Her eyes were wet with tears. "Take care of our son," she whispered. She put her arms around Taly and held him against her. Grove came behind her and the three of them rocked together. Then the parents broke away.

"No," Taly said. "Mom! Dad! Don't do this! I can protect us!"

The sight of their young son made the parents' faces crumple with love and pain.

"You can do so much," Grove said. "You can't do this."

Over Taly's head, Nelia turned her stricken eyes on Qui-Gon. "There's no time. Go. Please. Take him." Her voice ended in a sob.

Siri put her hand on Taly's shoulder. "Come on, Taly." She led him to Qui-Gon's swoop.

"Are you sure I cannot convince you to join us? Or two of us can stay with you."

"Go," Grove said. "Now."

Qui-Gon rested his strong gaze on Nelia. "I will protect him."

She nodded but did not speak. Tears streaked her face.

The Jedi felt the surge in the dark side of the Force. A warning. He was close.

"Hold on to me, Taly," Qui-Gon said kindly. "We will be traveling very fast."

They took off, keeping their acceleration low so as not to make noise. Then Qui-Gon quickly dipped down into a lower space lane so that they would not be visible from the building. Taly's parents disappeared from sight.

He felt the boy behind him, holding onto his tunic. He felt the cloth dampen with the boy's tears.

5

They made a clean getaway in the Republic cruiser. The city of Ciran retreated to a small yellow spot in a wide landscape. Then Cirrus became a yellowish round shape surrounded by clouds. In another few minutes, they were zooming through stars.

Adi piloted the ship. Qui-Gon set a course for Coruscant. Obi-Wan sat, watching Siri and Taly.

Siri did not speak. She moved about the cabin, close to Taly. She placed a small thermal blanket on his knees. Moments later she gave him something to eat and drink. Taly did not touch them. He held the blanket around his small body and stared at the ground.

Finally Siri came and sat beside him. She leaned forward and spoke to him gently. Obi-Wan could not hear her words but he saw by her posture how careful she was trying to be. He saw, gradually, how Taly's neck muscles relaxed, how his fingers no longer clutched the blanket with the same desperate grip.

Siri slipped something out of her utility belt. Obi-Wan recognized the warming crystal Siri always carried, deep blue with a star in the center. She handed it to Taly and he closed his fist around it, smiling at how it warmed his hand.

Siri drew her legs up underneath her and sat next to Taly, not too close, but not too far away.

Was this the Siri he knew? Hardly. Obi-Wan hadn't known she possessed such delicacy. Siri was never delicate. She said what she meant and she felt a great impatience for those who did not. She didn't like emotional reactions, she hated delays, she never waited on anyone or expected to be waited on. She liked to do everything herself.

These were the things he knew about her. But he did not know this. He hadn't realized she knew exactly what to do for a wounded child.

Suddenly Qui-Gon leaned over the nav console. "Unidentified cruiser coming up fast."

"I'll increase speed." Adi pushed the controls.

"He's speeding up," Qui-Gon said.

"You think it's our bounty hunter?"

"I have no doubt. And by the looks of that cruiser, he might be able to outmaneuver us. It's a SoroSuub light freighter."

Adi's mouth set grimly. "Nobody outmaneuvers me."

Qui-Gon gave a wry smile. "I didn't mean to suggest it. Deflector shields down." The Republic cruiser was an agile craft, but it was built to ferry diplomats and serve as a base for high-level meetings. Adi was an excellent pilot, but she would not be able to hold out against a heavily armed SoroSuub for very long.

By the posture of her shoulders, he knew exactly when she admitted this to herself. "Find us a safe port nearby, just in case."

Qui-Gon began to search the star chart on the nav computer. "We're close to Quadrant Seven," he said.

"I know," Adi said. "But what about a planet?"

"The planet's name *is* Quadrant Seven," Qui-Gon explained. "It's not in the Republic — it doesn't have a Senator and it's not particularly friendly to outlanders, but it doesn't forbid them, either." Qui-Gon entered the coordinates into the nav computer.

Adi pushed the ship to a faster speed. Obi-Wan and Siri got up and moved into the cockpit.

Taly followed. He leaned in close to the nav screen, sending a bluish light onto his features. "He's going to catch us," he said.

Qui-Gon met Adi's gaze. They both knew the boy was right.

Laser cannonfire thundered around the ship, rocking it. Taly gripped the console.

Adi kept the ship moving. She could not maneuver the way she would like, but she was able to swerve to avoid the next barrage. It boomed harmlessly in space.

"This is how he works," Taly said. "He uses everything. He never stops. He has blasters and grenades and missiles and . . . everything. I beat him, and that made him mad, because I'm just a kid. He won't let me go this time."

Qui-Gon looked at Taly. He had put the battle in terms of a young boy, but it made sense. Qui-Gon felt it, too, through his connection to the Living Force. This bounty hunter went beyond determination. This was a grudge.

"What should we do?" Adi asked. Her voice was perfectly calm despite the cannonfire that shook the ship. But Qui-Gon knew the situation must be dire, because Adi never asked him what to do.

Suddenly, a large blow rocked the ship.

"We've lost the horizontal stabilizer," Adi said. "It's affected the hyperdrive."

"We must send off the salon pod," Qui-Gon said. "He might think we escaped on it."

"But why would he fall for it?" Taly asked.

"Because then we're going to crash this ship," Qui-Gon said.

CHAPTER 6

"Maybe you'd better fill me in on this one," Adi said drily. "After all, I'm the pilot."

"This ship has a double-reinforced cargo hold," Qui-Gon said. "The work was done in order to protect a shipment of vertex on its last mission. So if we were hit there, it would cause minimal damage. We could make it look worse. We could trick him into thinking the ship was failing. Then we eject the salon pod. He knows that salon pods on these cruisers are capable of long space flights." Qui-Gon leveled his gaze at Adi. "Can you do it?"

She would know what he was asking. Adi could be high-handed at times. She could be dismissive of other ideas than her own. But they had worked together often enough to be able to put their minds in sync when they needed to.

"Yes."

Qui-Gon turned. "Obi-Wan, Siri, Taly, get all the soft material you can and bring them to the cockpit. Flotation devices, roll-up sleep couches, bedding, pillows, cushions. Fast."

Obi-Wan, Siri, and Taly dashed out of the cockpit. The Republic cruiser was built as a diplomatic ship. There were plenty of cabins to raid. Within minutes, the cockpit had filled up with soft bedding. Qui-Gon directed the three to place it around the walls and hard surfaces as carefully as they could.

"We're going to have take a missile blow," he told the others. "Brace yourself."

Adi maneuvered the ship so that the blow would fall on the cargo hold. It would take perfect timing and a lot of guesswork. She had to make the bounty hunter think that he had outmaneuvered them and struck the death blow.

The ship screamed through space, twisting like a corkscrew. The Force filled the cabin as Adi concentrated, beads of perspiration on her high forehead. They saw the flash as the laser cannon boomed. They had less than a split-second to prepare.

The blast shook the ship and blew them like durasheets through the cabin. They bounced off the cushions and mattresses. Qui-Gon felt helpless as his wrist slammed against the edge of the console. He pulled in the Force to give him stability and balance. Adi crawled to the pilot chair.

"I didn't expect to do quite this good a job," she muttered, gripping the controls.

"Jettison some smoke," Qui-Gon said.

Adi put the ship into a death spiral. She released the salon pod. They were close to a planet now, twisting down toward it.

Qui-Gon had his eyes on the radar. "He's not chasing the pod. Not yet."

Adi looked at him worriedly. "He's waiting for us to flame out or crash."

Qui-Gon nodded. "So let's crash."

Adi gripped the controls. Siri strapped Taly down and belted down cushions around him. She and Obi-Wan covered themselves as best they could.

The ship was screaming now, belching smoke. But Adi still had control. She mimicked a dying ship, narrowing the circles until Qui-Gon had to close his eyes against the dizziness he felt. He opened them once to see the surface of the planet looming. He closed them again quickly.

"Here we go!" Adi shouted.

He never knew how she did it. The grace and precision of it were amazing. She was able to pull up slightly at the last minute, enough for the ship to shudder into a modified crash landing instead of slamming into the planet's surface. But from the upper atmosphere, it would look like a crash. She jettisoned the fuel early so that it sent up a fireball. The smoke would cover their escape.

Qui-Gon took out his lightsaber and cut a hole through the wall. Obi-Wan joined him, then Siri and Adi. Taly stood back, his eyes huge with shock.

Qui-Gon picked up Taly and jumped out the hole after the others. They took shelter behind some rocks as the ship exploded.

"Now what?" Siri asked.

"Let's start with the basics," Qui-Gon said. "I'd say we need to locate new transportation."

Taly still wore an expression of shock. "Don't you Jedi take a minute to recover?"

"He took off after the pod, but we should still take precautions," Adi said. "I think Taly should remain in hiding with Siri and Obi-Wan. We don't want to leave a trail. We know there is more than one bounty hunter involved."

"Good point," Qui-Gon said.

They walked toward town. The road was dusty and deserted, winding through a rocky canyon. Halfway there, Adi suddenly stopped. She leaned over and pressed her hand against the ground.

"There's water close to here," she said. "Follow me."

She took off through the rocks. They followed, Taly sometimes slipping and helped by Siri. Adi led them up a stony ridge and then down again. The air smelled fresher. Around a large boulder was a small, bubbling spring.

"A water source if you need it," she said. She glanced around. "There are caves around us. I can feel them."

She walked to a cleft in the rocks. Qui-Gon never would have noticed it. He would have thought it was a shadow. Adi melted inside and they saw only her hand beckon them.

It was a cave, small and snug. Although the sand was cool and damp, farther into the cave it was dry.

"A perfect hiding place," Adi said. "Invisible from the air. Easy to exit and close to town." She slipped off her survival pack. "We'll be back for you as soon as we locate transport. You'll be comfortable here."

Siri looked around the cave dubiously. "If you say so."

Qui-Gon couldn't help smiling at Siri. "We'll return soon," he promised.

Qui-Gon and Adi left the cave and continued on the road to the city of Settlement 5. The city had no outskirts. It simply rose in the middle of a convergence of roads. There seemed to be no green spaces, no culture centers or amusements, just businesses and homes, all built on a grid of streets and lanes.

The city was more like an overgrown village than a sophisticated center. Qui-Gon and Adi walked through the streets, their hoods up, trying to blend in. It wasn't hard. They were taller than the average Quadrant Seven, but that wasn't a problem. All the Quadrant Sevens wore practical and neutral-colored robes, just as the Jedi did. Most of them walked with their hoods over their faces. Qui-Gon felt anonymous in the crowd, and he soon realized why.

"They're *all* trying to blend in," he murmured to Adi. "Even if they recognize us as outlanders, they won't show it."

Usually in a main city of a world in the Core or Mid-Rim, there were plenty of opportunities to buy or rent speeders, and often dealers in spaceworthy cruisers clustered around the landing platforms of the city. But there was a strange absence of such dealers on this planet. It took Adi and

Qui-Gon some time to find a seller of speeders tucked away down a narrow lane off a secondary road.

A laserboard outside discreetly flashed specials. "Nothing spaceworthy," Qui-Gon said. "But no doubt he can tell us where to purchase a ship."

They walked inside. The dwellers of Quadrant Seven were humanoid, with small, pointed ears and short, whiskery antennae that gave the appearance of bristly hair but were finely attuned to disturbances in the air. The dealer turned, his antennae quivering.

He didn't ask them what they wanted, or if he could help them. He just stood, waiting for them to speak.

"We're looking for a space cruiser," Qui-Gon said.

"I don't sell that here," the dealer said.

"We thought you could tell us where in Settlement Five we could purchase one."

"Nowhere. There's no call for selling of space cruisers. Quadrants don't like to travel out of their own atmosphere."

"But surely," Qui-Gon said patiently, "there is a way to get off planet."

"Well, of course there is."

Adi kept her tone even. "Maybe you could tell us what that is."

"Wait for the freighter. It comes once a month."

Qui-Gon felt his heart fall. "Once a month?"

The dealer seemed to feel that he had no need to elaborate.

"Can you tell us when it will stop again?" Adi asked.

The dealer consulted a calendar on his datapad. "Ah, that would be market day."

"And market day is . . ."

"In five standard days time."

Qui-Gon took out his comlink. "Can you tell us where on Quadrant Seven we could find a space cruiser? We could contact them and —"

"Ah, that would be Settlement Twenty-three. That's where you'd be able to bargain for a ship. But you can't contact them by comlink. There's a BlocNet on Quadrant Seven. Comlinks are licensed. Ordinary citizens aren't allowed to carry them, just emergency personnel. Your comlink won't work here."

"But why outlaw comlinks?" Adi asked.

"Don't believe in 'em. Comlinks make distances shorter. And when distances get shorter, problems get bigger. We like to slow things down on Quadrant Seven. Which reminds me, you need a permit to send a HoloNet message off planet. It will be monitored and archived, too."

"And who has access to the archives?" Adi asked.

"Everyone. Makes beings nicer if they know they can't send out messages that aren't public."

Adi and Qui-Gon stared at each other in frustration. That meant if they sent a message to the Temple, everyone would be able to see it. The bounty hunters could trace them.

"Can we buy a speeder to travel to Settlement Twenty-three?" Qui-Gon asked.

"Sure. But you have to apply for a permit. All out-landers do."

"How long will it take to get a permit?"

"Hard to say. Could be a week."

Adi was becoming used to the dealer's way of talk-ing. "Or . . . ?

"Could be a month. Hard to say."

"This is ridiculous," Adi muttered. "What a way to run a planet."

"We haven't had a war in five hundred and seventy-three years," the dealer said. "Don't have toxic pools or chemical air. Everybody pretty much gets along. That doesn't sound too ridiculous, does it?"

Adi just sighed.

"If I were you, I'd wait for the freighter. Quadrant Seven is a nice place to visit. Of course we don't have much in the way of hotels or cafés. And we don't go in for amuse-ments the way they do in other places. There's not much to do. But still."

"Look, we don't have time to wait," Qui-Gon said. "Can't you find a way to help us?"

"Nope." The dealer's face was still blandly polite. He would be friendly, but not help them. That much was clear.

They walked out of the shop.

"Looks like we're waiting for the freighter," Adi said.

"We'll just have to lay low. We could send a coded communication to the Temple. . . ."

"But why risk it?" Adi completed the sentence. "If by some chance the bounty hunter searches the planet, that's the first place he'd investigate. Even a coded message would stand out."

"We can canvass the area, look to see if anyone owns a ship and try to buy it," Qui-Gon said.

Adi nodded. "It doesn't appear that Quadrant Sevens travel, but we might get lucky."

"It's only five days," Qui-Gon said. "The assassination will take place in a week. This can all work, if nothing else goes wrong."

He felt the dark side surge as a warning just as Adi pulled him back from walking out into the watery sunlight. The bounty hunter was striding by on the street, his pale eyes flicking into the shadows.

"Something else just went wrong," Adi said.

CHAPTER 7

"Let's follow him," Adi murmured. "Better to know where he is — and perhaps we'll learn something."

Qui-Gon nodded. They melted into the crowd in the street. It was rare that a being knew when he was being followed by a Jedi. They were able to use the Force to direct objects to move into their path if someone turned to look behind them. They were able to move before their prey could track their steps. After a short time, the Jedi were able to so absorb their quarry's way of moving that they could predict it and easily avoid discovery.

The bounty hunter was good. He was careful. Yet he was no match for them. Adi and Qui-Gon followed him easily as he walked to the opposite edge of Settlement 5 and then struck out across the hills and rocks.

This area was even more rugged than where they'd left Obi-Wan and Siri. They trailed him through a series of small, deep canyons. The boulders offered plenty of hiding places. At last he slipped into a narrow opening and disappeared. Qui-Gon and Adi carefully moved forward. Positioning themselves behind an outcropping, they peered into the opening.

It led to a canyon that was just a cleft in the land-scape. They recognized the bounty hunter's light freighter. Next to it was a slightly larger ship. Together they took up nearly the entire width of the canyon.

The bounty hunter disappeared into the larger ship. The ramp was down, and Qui-Gon and Adi slowly made their way there. With a glance at each other, they agreed to try to observe what was going on. It was worth the risk.

They crept up the ramp and slipped inside the ship. They heard raised voices coming from the cockpit.

Good, Qui-Gon thought. If a group was arguing, they would be too distracted to stay alert.

Tall and graceful, Adi moved ahead of him down the hall, her boots soundless on the polished floor. She beck-oned to him. She had found a vent at eye level, in a storage room right off the cockpit. Qui-Gon could see quite clearly into the next room.

His heart fell. There were five bounty hunters in the cockpit, including the one chasing them. Among them was one he recognized — Gorm the Dissolver. He was a formidable presence, dwarfing the others in his plated armor and helmet. Created by Arkanian Renegades, he was half-bio, half-droid. His bio parts were made up of six different aliens. His droid components allowed him to be a nearly invincible killing machine. Gorm's tracking skill was legendary and his merciless attacks were spoken of in whispers in spaceports throughout the galaxy.

All of these bounty hunters in one place, for one assassination? Qui-Gon wondered again who the target could be.

"We've only got a week," one of the bounty hunters said. It was a humanoid woman, small and compact, dressed in a leather tunic and leggings. Her fair hair was twisted in many braids that fell to her shoulders. She appeared to be completely ordinary, if you didn't notice the firepower strapped to her waist, her wrist gauntlets with an array of weapons systems, or the armored kneepads she wore. By the look of her armor, Qui-Gon guessed she was a Mandalorian, or at least that she had somehow procured some of the warrior army's famous weaponry. "You shouldn't have blasted that escape pod, Magus," she went on. "Now we don't know for sure if you got the kid."

The bounty hunter who had chased them on Cirrus turned slowly and rested his steely gaze on the female.

"Don't give me that black-hole look, Magus," she said. "You know I'm right. We need proof that the kid has been neutralized. If he's still alive, he could compromise the mission. I don't mind pulling this off, but I don't want anybody to know I was involved. Those Senatorial committees can get touchy about political assassinations."

"We're only a week away from our hits," another bounty hunter said. He was a tall creature with green-tinged skin and a cranial horn on top of his head. "I for one don't relish the thought of assassinating a world leader if security is waiting for me. And we've got twenty targets. That's twenty times the security."

Qui-Gon and Adi exchanged a glance. *Twenty* planetary leaders?

"I told you, they won't have their regular security," Magus said.

"We still have no way of knowing how much this kid knows and who he's alerted," the female bounty hunter continued.

"You promised they wouldn't be expecting us, that we'd have the element of surprise," the third bounty hunter said to Magus. He wore a greasy cloak and his leggings were thick with grime. Tufts of wiry hair stood out on his head like horns. On his grimy face gills flapped open and closed with his breathing. He looked like a large, unkempt fish. A name floated into Qui-Gon's head. *Raptor.* This could be the bounty hunter he'd been hearing about, the one who was willing to take any job, no matter how dangerous or cruel. "That's one reason we agreed. Well — that and the fee. But if security gets tipped off, I'm heading back to the Core and picking up another job. What does our employer say?"

Magus rose slowly. If he was bothered by the dissension in the others, it wasn't apparent. "Our employer leaves the details to me. As you should."

"We did that," the being with the cranial horn said. "And now we don't know if the kid is dead or not. We don't know if he blabbed yet or not. We don't know if he's on his way to the Senate to testify."

"I heard you the first time, Pilot," Magus said, the anger now clear in his tone.

"Really? Because it doesn't seem like you're listening," the female said irritably.

"Lunasa is right," Raptor said. "You've got a problem listening to any voice but your own."

Magus slammed a vibroblade down on the table. "Enough whining!" he exploded. With the exception of Gorm, the bounty hunters all looked unnerved. "I said I would take care of the boy. First we need to complete the preparations we discussed. There's still much to be done, and we're wasting time here."

Without waiting for agreement, Magus simply strode off. Qui-Gon and Adi had to scurry back along the corridor to avoid him. He strode down the ramp and headed for his own ship.

"Who elected him king, I'd like to know," Lunasa muttered.

"He recruited us," Pilot said. "But the employer talks to me, too. I can go to him anytime." A bragging note had entered his voice.

"Whoa, and that makes you *so* special," Raptor said.

"I'm keeping track of what Magus does," Pilot said huffily. "That's all I'm saying."

"Shut up." Gorm spoke for the first time. "Let's go."

It took them a moment, no doubt because they didn't want to appear to follow anyone's orders, but the bounty hunters began to make preparations for departure. Pilot headed for the controls. Lunasa worked on the nav computer. The one Qui-Gon suspected of being Raptor shrugged and took off down the corridor, presumably to his own cabin. Qui-Gon and Adi ducked into a storage room.

"Twenty leaders? It's much bigger than we thought," Adi said. "We have to find out who they're targeting."

"And *why*," Qui-Gon added. "If we find the why, we can discover who hired them." He thought quickly. "We should stay aboard."

"But Taly —"

"Obi-Wan and Siri can protect him. They are well hidden. We can return for them. There's no way off the planet for five days. Magus knows that as well — that's why he's leaving. No doubt he plans to return, but we can be back by then."

Adi frowned. "I don't like leaving the three of them."

"Uncovering the plot will help Taly more than our presence," Qui-Gon said. "I don't like leaving them, either. But I feel Obi-Wan and Siri can handle this."

Adi nodded slowly. "Agreed."

"Once we're out of the Quadrant Seven atmosphere, we can send them a message," Qui-Gon said. "Incoming messages aren't recorded. It's a risk to leave, but . . ."

". . . we have to take it," Adi said.

They felt the thrust of the engines. The ship lifted into the air.

"Hey!" they heard Lunasa call. "Magus is staying!"

"He never tells us what he's doing," Pilot said.

"I guess he's going for the kid after all," Lunasa said.

Adi and Qui-Gon glanced at each other. The ship was already climbing to the upper atmosphere. It was too late to get off.

CHAPTER 8

"They should have been back by now."

Siri kept her voice low, but Taly seemed off in another world. He sat at the entrance to the cave, his arms around his knees. Occasionally he would dip his head down and stare at the ground.

"I know." Obi-Wan wanted to argue with her, but he didn't have a good feeling about the length of time Qui-Gon and Adi had been gone.

"I should go look for them."

"They told us to stay here."

Siri shook her head impatiently. "Obi-Wan, in all my years of knowing you, I can't tell you how many times you've told me what I *should* be doing."

"Well, somebody has to," Obi-Wan said with a grin.

But Siri didn't crack a smile. "They could be in trouble."

"Or they could be negotiating for a starship. Or they could be contacting the Temple. Or they could be on their way back. They could be doing a thousand things. None of which are our concern. Our concern is Taly. They told us both to protect him. So here we stay."

Siri's jaw set stubbornly. She stared stonily out into the landscape.

Taly suddenly rose and came back to stand with them. "I have a proposition for you," he said.

Obi-Wan wanted to smile. There was something so touching about Taly. Here was this slender, small boy who seemed ready to take on the world. Sometimes the lost look in his eyes made him look like a child. Yet sometimes he talked like an adult. Obi-Wan had no idea how much of Taly's confidence was bravery and how much was bravado. All he knew was that he admired him.

"Let's hear it," Siri said.

"I want you to let me go," Taly said.

"Let you go?" Obi-Wan repeated, incredulous.

Taly nodded. "I've been thinking about it. My uncle is a subplanetary engineer on the planet Qexis. It's a high-security planet with only one spaceport. It's in the Outer Rim. Nobody really knows about it except tech-heads. It's a total research planet. He'd hide me for as long as it takes. And you could tell my parents where I'm heading and they could meet me there. I could make my way there."

"You could make your way there?" Obi-Wan tried unsuccessfully to keep his voice from rising.

Taly looked at Siri. "Does he always repeat what people say?"

Siri nodded. "Yeah."

"Taly, there's no way we're going to let you go," Obi-Wan said. "That's preposterous. What makes you think you could get to the Outer Rim by yourself? You're just a kid!"

"Nobody notices a kid," Taly said. "I can do it, I know I can. It's just a question of getting from Point A to Point B. The bounty hunters think I'm dead."

"You don't know that for sure. We tricked one of them. We don't know if it worked. That's why we're still in hiding."

"That's what gives me a head start," Taly said. "Look, you know as well as I do that if I testify to those Senators, I'm dead."

"That's not true," Obi-Wan said, shocked. "They'll protect you."

"You trust the Senate?" Taly gave a bark of a laugh. "And you call *me* a kid?"

Obi-Wan shook his head. He wasn't going to argue with Taly. He shot Siri an exasperated look, but to his surprise, Siri was looking at Taly thoughtfully.

"You know it's true," Taly said, turning to Siri. "They won't care about me once I testify. Sure, they'll give me new ID docs. But they won't protect me or my parents, not really. But if I don't testify, maybe the bounty hunters will leave me alone."

"Taly, they won't leave you alone," Obi-Wan said gently. "I'm sorry to say it. But you'll always be a risk to them."

"Not after they do the assassination," Taly argued.

"Then they won't care. Or even if they care, they're not going to chase me for long. I'm not worth it. I can disappear." He turned back to Siri. "Okay, I'll make a deal with you. You can escort me to Qexis. Then leave me there. Pretend I escaped. You can save my life. You can save my parents. You *can.*"

"Taly, I'm sorry," Obi-Wan said.

"Siri?" Taly looked at her beseechingly.

Siri spoke through dry lips. "I'm sorry, too."

Taly stomped off to the front of the cave, a kid again. Obi-Wan looked at Siri.

"I could have used a little support," he said.

"What if he's right?" Siri asked.

"What if he's *right*?"

Siri rolled her eyes. "There you go again."

"There I . . . Siri, you can't be serious. You can't think that we could possibly let Taly go."

"No, of course not. But we *could* take him to Qexis. It *would* be a good place to hide. And the Senate *won't* protect him. Not the way they should. They just want what they want. Once he testifies, they won't care about him. He's not wrong, Obi-Wan."

"Sometimes I just don't understand you."

"I know."

"We can't defy the Senate. We can't defy the Jedi Council."

"We can. We just don't choose to. There are more options in life, Obi-Wan, than you seem able to imagine."

Siri's words stung. It was almost as though she felt sorry for him.

"Do I need to tell Qui-Gon and Adi about this?" Obi-Wan hated the way he sounded. Priggish. Pompous.

Siri turned her cool gaze on him, the color of an impossibly blue sea with hidden depths for the unwary. "If you like. Don't worry. I'll deliver Taly into the hands of the Senate. I'll do my duty. I always do."

Then she retreated from him, even though she stayed still and unmoving at his side.

The comlink message was full of static.

". . . trail of bounty hunters. . . . Stay where you are until we return . . ." Qui-Gon's voice was steady, but the transmission crackled. "A bounty hunter is on Quadrant Seven. Magus. Stay hidden. If we don't return . . ."

"Qui-Gon?"

"Freighter . . . landing platform . . . in five days time, midday. No other transport available —" The transmission cut out.

"Did you get all that?" Siri asked.

"Stay hidden for five days. If they don't return, take the freighter off planet. And a bounty hunter is still looking for Taly."

"Magus." Siri looked over at where Taly was sleeping. "So he knows Taly is alive."

"Or suspects."

She did not say what he knew she wanted to say. Without their Masters, it would be easy to go to Qexis. They could take Taly away from this.

But those were not their orders. And they would do their duty.

CHAPTER 9

Siri didn't speak much. There was a tension between them now that Obi-Wan didn't understand. They had argued many times during their friendship. Why did this one make him feel so strained?

He hadn't realized before how much her steady friendship meant to him. She might mock him and annoy him, but he'd always known she respected him.

Now he wasn't sure.

The days passed slowly. The cave seemed smaller with each segment of passing time. Obi-Wan felt himself grow more silent with every passing hour. He felt himself tense whenever Siri brushed past. He felt like a fool, like a rule-following, dull, stupid apprentice who didn't dare to risk. He never felt like that when Siri wasn't around.

The tension between them grew, and he didn't understand it. Obi-Wan couldn't wait to get out of the cave.

They did what Jedi do when forced to remain in one place. They kept themselves limber with exercises. They meditated. They did not think of the future, only the present moment.

One would stand guard while the other went down to the spring for water. They saw no one and heard nothing. Every hour, they expected Qui-Gon and Adi to contact them. They both felt a responsibility to keep the atmosphere light. They didn't want to worry Taly.

For his part, Taly crunched on protein pellets and slept fitfully. He stopped eating much. Obi-Wan began to worry about him. He and Siri slept in shifts so that one of them would always be awake. He didn't think it impossible that Taly would try to slip away. He saw how Siri's eyes grew dark with worry when she looked at him.

"We just have to hang on," he said to her.

She was scratching patterns in the dirt floor of the cave with a stick. She didn't look up. "One of us should do some reconnaissance," she said. "We don't know what the road is like to Settlement Five, or how many kilometers it is."

"We have the coordinates and a map on our datapad."

"A map is not the territory. You've told me that yourself."

Yes, he had. It was a saying of Qui-Gon's. *Study the map, but do not trust it. A map is not the territory. Until your boots are on it, do not trust the ground.*

"Yes, that's true. But the settlement isn't far, and the road is well marked. I think we risk more by scouting it out. If our Masters thought we needed to do it, they would have told us. They've traveled the road."

Siri looked up. "Orders for the Jedi are not meant to be

literal. Padawans should use their own judgment. That is a Jedi rule, too."

"If situations change," Obi-Wan said. "Ours is the same." He hated this. He hated spouting Jedi rules to Siri as though he was a Master and she was a Padawan. He knew how much she hated it, too. But she pushed him to a place where he had to.

That night at the evening meal, Obi-Wan watched as Taly pushed his protein pellets away. "I want real food."

"We only have two more days to wait," Obi-Wan told him. "There will be food on the freighter. Until then you must take nourishment. You must be strong, Taly. You have a long way to go, and it would be illogical to weaken yourself now."

He watched as Taly took another protein pellet and nodded as he swallowed it.

"That's better."

The moon rose, and they rolled themselves into their thermal blankets. Obi-Wan heard Taly's breathing slow and deepen.

In a few minutes he heard a noise. Siri crawled over to his side. She held out a palm full of protein pellets. "I found these behind a rock."

Obi-Wan frowned. "They must be Taly's. I don't understand. Why won't he eat?"

Siri tossed the pellets toward the rear of the cave. "Because these taste like rocks with a frosting of sand, that's why. We're used to them. He's not. He's just a kid, Obi-Wan."

"He's a very smart kid who knows how much trouble he's in," Obi-Wan said. "We're leaving in two days. Why would he starve himself?"

"Because he's scared and he misses his parents and everything's out of his control," Siri said impatiently. "Because beings don't always behave *logically*. This is the Living Force. It's unpredictable."

"I hate unpredictability," Obi-Wan said.

Siri smiled. "I know."

"So what should we do?"

"Are you asking me? That's a first," Siri teased.

"Yes, I'm asking you."

"I don't know. Let me think about it. I'll take the first watch."

Siri crawled to the entrance to the cave and positioned herself against the curve of the wall. He watched her curl into the wall as if it were the most comfortable of cushions. The moon was so big that night that he could see her profile illuminated, the crystal clarity of her eyes, the gleam of her hair. She managed to look both alert and perfectly comfortable.

For the first time in days, Obi-Wan slept deeply.

When he awoke, Siri was gone.

CHAPTER 10

Dawn was still at least an hour away. It was cold in the cave. Obi-Wan wrapped his thermal blanket around his shoulders and sat at the cave opening. Even if he had wanted to search for Siri, he wouldn't leave Taly.

The light was shifting to purple when Siri reappeared, running soundlessly toward the cave, never making a wrong step even on the stony ground. When she caught sight of Obi-Wan she slowed. He saw her shoulders rise slightly, as if bracing herself for his attack.

She crouched down in front of him and removed a small sack from her tunic. "I got food for Taly," she said. "A muja muffin, some bread, some fruit."

"But I'm carrying all the credits," Obi-Wan said.

"I traded for them," Siri said. "My warming crystal. I sold it to a vendor who was opening up his shop early."

She looked embarrassed. She had sacrificed her most prized possession for a boy she hardly knew. It was a gesture full of sentiment. In the past, Obi-Wan would have thought it unlike her. Now, he knew better.

"Go ahead," she said. "Yell at me."

He didn't say anything. He'd always admired Siri for

her fierceness. He had never known how strong her connection to the Living Force was. She always seemed to hold herself above other beings. Now he saw that her brusqueness was a kind of distance she kept, but even so, she was watching. Feeling.

"He'll like these," Obi-Wan said. "It was a good idea. You can go to sleep now. I'll keep watch."

"I can't sleep," Siri said gruffly. "Mind if I sit for awhile?"

Obi-Wan moved over to make room. Siri sat next to him.

"It's cold," she said. "But it's going to be a nice day."

He threw the blanket over her shoulders so that it was covering them both. He felt her leg against his, her breath against his ear. Warmth spread through him. He saw the sun begin to touch the rocks outside.

"One more day," she said. "I hope Qui-Gon and Adi make it back in time."

"If they don't, we'll be okay," Obi-Wan said. "We can handle anything if we're together."

"I know." He felt the whisper against his skin. They sat together and watched the light come up.

Qui-Gon and Adi did not return, and they did not send another message. Obi-Wan and Siri began to pack up their survival kits. They would have to do this on their own.

"If the bounty hunter is still on Quadrant Seven, he'll be watching to see if we board," Siri said. "We'll have to sneak on somehow."

"Qui-Gon always says that when you're trying to sneak in someplace, go where the food is," Obi-Wan said. "They load it separately through cargo, and security is sometimes pretty loose. Let's try there first."

"Sounds like a plan," Siri said. "Ready, Taly?"

Taly shouldered his pack. Once again, Obi-Wan was struck by how resolute he could look. He had accepted Siri's gift of food gratefully and had tried to share. Obi-Wan and Siri had both taken a small piece of fruit but insisted he eat most of the fresh food. He had been more cheerful after that. It wasn't so much the food, Obi-Wan thought, as the caring that had improved his mood and given him hope. Siri had been so right. He had things to learn from her that went beyond a new fighting stance. He had things to learn about the heart. About giving.

"I'm ready," Taly said.

Siri put her hands on his shoulders and squatted so that she was eye-level with him. "Here's the most important thing, Taly. You have to do what we say. Your safety depends on it."

He nodded. "I will."

Obi-Wan could see that he meant it. Siri had won his trust.

They set off. Because it was market day, the road was crowded with beings heading into Settlement 5. That was lucky. The crowds gave them plenty of cover.

The marketplace was set up around the landing platform, which was another lucky break. Stalls and vendors crowded the square where ramps and lift tubes led to the landing platform several stories above. Siri, Obi-Wan, and Taly blended in with the others in their plain robes and hoods. Siri and Obi-Wan kept their gazes constantly moving but they did not catch a glimpse of the bounty hunter. Nor did the Force give them a warning.

The freighter was docked and ready for loading. One passenger ramp was already down. It would be easy to board and search for seats, but Obi-Wan thought it best to wait until the last possible moment.

They saw metal bins being carried to the back ramp, fresh fruit and vegetables spilling over the top. Obi-Wan watched for several minutes as they milled through the crowd, pretending to study the wares set up in booths and spread out on tables. The bins were carried by workers who plodded back and forth up the ramp. When they disappeared inside the freighter, they were usually gone for a minute or so. That would easily give Obi-Wan, Siri, and Taly a chance to pick up a bin and bring it aboard. If they timed it right, they could pull it off.

Obi-Wan nudged Siri. "There. They're loading the fresh food. If we pick up a bin we could get aboard. Nobody is really watching."

Siri nodded. Then suddenly she paled. "He's here."

"Where?"

"I feel him." Siri's gaze raked the crowd. "There."

Obi-Wan looked where Siri's gaze was resting. Magus was across the square. He stood in a clever spot, right where the sun was in shadow, behind a bin of vegetables that were a popular item for shoppers. It would have been hard to pick him out if Siri hadn't felt his presence.

"It's all right," Obi-Wan said. "He's searching the crowd. Now's our chance."

Siri swallowed. She kept her head down. "He's standing with the vendor I bought the food from. He knows we're here, Obi-Wan!"

Obi-Wan looked again. He realized that vendor standing next to Magus was also watching the crowd. Magus was smart. While the vendor concentrated on the passenger ramp, his own flinty gaze roamed. Now Obi-Wan saw how the bounty hunter kept his eye on the cargo ramp as well as the food ramp. There were now less than a dozen bins to carry. Time was running out.

"What are we going to do?" Taly asked.

Obi-Wan knew it was hopeless. There was no way they could board without Magus spotting them. No matter how cleverly they tried. Yet staying on the planet wasn't a good idea. Sooner or later, Magus would find them. And it would probably be sooner.

The panic in Taly's eyes made Obi-Wan angry. They had to protect him. They had to get him to a place that was safe.

"If he's here, that means his ship is unguarded," Obi-Wan said.

A flash illuminated Siri's blue gaze. "You want to steal his ship?"

"The freighter is due to leave in five minutes. We've got to find it first."

"It will be close," Siri guessed.

"Come on."

They threaded through the crowd with a purpose now, but were careful to move with the flowing surge. Obi-Wan checked out the possibilities. It would make sense for Magus to keep the cruiser near. Usually there was a holding pen for star cruisers near landing platforms. He hadn't noticed one here, but there should be one somewhat close.

"There," Siri breathed.

Around a corner, down an alley, a clearly marked space. It was empty but for one cruiser, the light freighter they knew belonged to Magus. They hurried toward the durasteel gate.

There was no time to lose. Obi-Wan cut a hole in the gate with his lightsaber and they squeezed through.

He prowled around the outside of the ship. Siri did the same.

"There should be an exterior control panel for the ramp," he said.

"Here it is." Taly's voice came from underneath the ship. "Sometimes these SoroSuubs are refitted with foiling devices. I can cross the wires and tinker with the controls here. . . ."

"Taly, let me," Obi-Wan urged.

The ramp slid down. "No need." Taly slid out and jumped up, dusting off his hands, a huge grin on his face. "We're done."

They ran up the ramp. Obi-Wan slid into the pilot seat.

"Wait." Taly ducked underneath the control panel. "Let's make sure there's no locking device. I can bypass the access code."

"Are you sure?" Siri asked.

"Easy as cutting through air." Taly took a small servodriver from his utility belt. "Standard security devices . . . Code deactivated . . . Remote tracking device cut . . . Okay. Let's go."

Obi-Wan fired up the engines. He kept the engine speed down until they were safely away from the city. Then he blasted into the upper atmosphere.

He grinned at Siri. They made it.

"Set the course for Coruscant."

"Course set."

Minutes passed. Siri watched the computer screen avidly. There was still a chance they could be followed.

"Setting hyperdrive," Obi-Wan said. He flicked the controls. Space rushed toward them in a shower of stars. They were free.

With a sigh of satisfaction, Taly leaned back in his seat.

"I bet I'm really starting to get on that guy's nerves," he said.

CHAPTER 11

The problem with eavesdropping, Qui-Gon thought, was that it required beings who liked one another enough to exchange information. He and Adi had hoped to over-hear more of the bounty hunters' plans, but as soon as their argument was over and the ship blasted off, they all retreated to separate areas of the ship and did not speak. They passed one another in the corridors, they met in the galley scrounging for food, they bumped into one another at close quarters, but all Qui-Gon and Adi heard was an occasional grunt or grumble of, "Blast your stinking carcass, stay out of my way."

They had been on the ship for three days and had learned nothing. They didn't know their destination, and they didn't know the bounty hunters' targets. They had moved from hiding place to hiding place, from storage compartment to empty stateroom and back again, and at last found what they felt was safe refuge in the small escape pod compartment.

When night fell, the sound of snoring penetrated even the thick door on the compartment. Pilot slept across the hall.

"We've got to do something," Adi said. "We could be landing soon. Not to mention that I'm going to go out of my mind."

"Meditation not working?"

Adi cocked an eyebrow at him. "Very amusing, Qui-Gon. You forget that I am the Jedi without a sense of humor. We need a plan. Something logical."

Qui-Gon smiled. "Why don't we just sneak around some more and see what we can turn up?"

Adi regarded him gravely. "Sounds good."

"I have an idea," Qui-Gon continued. "Pilot said he's in touch with their employer. And that he's keeping records on Magus. Maybe he's kept things he shouldn't."

They listened to the snoring that thundered down the corridor.

"He does sound like a heavy sleeper," Adi said. "Let's go."

Together they crept into Pilot's cabin. He stirred but didn't wake, instead sighing and turning over on his sleep couch. One long arm flopped over the side, his knuckles grazing the floor.

Adi nudged Qui-Gon. Pilot had dislodged his pillow. Now his head was half-on, half-off, and they saw a small datapad underneath the pillow.

Slowly, Adi leaned over. She slid her hand toward the pillow.

Pilot grunted. Adi froze.

Slowly, bit by tiny bit, she moved her hand underneath

to grab the edge of the datapad. As if she had all the time in the world, she slid it out from underneath.

Pilot snuggled more deeply into the blankets.

Adi and Qui-Gon bent over the datapad. Quickly, they accessed its files. They were all in code. They accessed the last file used. It was correspondence between Pilot and someone whose name was also in code. But Pilot had made an additional notation and had not coded it.

20 targets. mtg day one set.

Pilot began to stir. He was waking this time. They saw him lift his arm. He began to pat underneath the pillow, eyes still closed, to reassure himself that the datapad was still there.

Adi moved noiselessly across the floor. She had to bend over him, only centimeters from his cheek, as she slid the datapad back in place. Wrinkling her nose, she jerked her chin toward the door. Time to go.

Moving slowly, she withdrew from the sleep couch. Suddenly, Pilot's hand shot out and grabbed her tunic.

"Where do you think you're going?" His eyes snapped open and confusion shot him to a sitting position. "And who are you?"

With a quick movement Adi dislodged herself from his grasp and kicked him in the chest, sending him back across the sleep couch with an *oof.*

She and Qui-Gon hurtled out the door, drawing their lightsabers. As they ran, an alarm began to clang. There must have been an alert button right near the sleep couch.

They heard pounding footsteps behind them. Lunasa must have slept half-dressed. She still wore a tunic and boots, but she was bare-legged and her hair was matted from sleep and stood out in dark wisps around her head. A small rocket whistled toward them and then blaster fire richocheted in the air. Qui-Gon sliced through the rocket while Adi deflected the blaster fire.

From the opposite side of the corridor, Gorm the Dissolver strode toward them, fire shooting from the blasters in both hands. Adi and Qui-Gon kept constantly circling. Pilot had advanced out from his stateroom and joined the melee.

"Any ideas?" Adi muttered to Qui-Gon as she twirled, deflecting fire. The corridor was filled with smoke.

"Seems like a good time to escape," Qui-Gon said. "How about the pod?"

An ominous *clacking* came to their ears. Droidekas suddenly rolled down the corridor, unfurling to their full, deadly length.

"The pod sounds good," Adi replied.

Qui-Gon and Adi moved grimly forward.

Qui-Gon moved to the left, trying to get Gorm between him and the droidekas. But the two had excellent homing devices and moved accordingly. Gorm kept on a steady pace, thumping forward, blasting with a repeating rifle.

Qui-Gon saw that he had to end this. Between the droidekas and the bounty hunters, he saw a danger of being wounded or captured.

He surged forward, cutting off the leg of a droideka

and almost getting clipped by blaster fire in the process. The droideka lost its center of balance and spun. Blaster fire peppered out in a random pattern, almost hitting Lunasa. She yelled and hit the ground, still firing at the Jedi. Raptor almost got in the way, and had to leap over Lunasa, placing himself between Gorm and the Jedi.

All this happened in just a few seconds.

Qui-Gon and Adi leaped through the door of the escape pod hatch. They accessed the door and tumbled inside. They could hear the bounty hunters pounding after them.

"The airlock!" Adi yelled.

Qui-Gon hit it. He quickly activated the prelaunch sequence. The door thudded with the impact of blaster bolts.

"Not a grenade, you idiot!" Lunasa shouted. "You could damage the —"

They never knew who the idiot had been, but the grenade exploded. At the same moment the escape pod shot out into space, rocking with the motion of the grenade blast. They heard shrapnel pepper the shell of the pod, but it did not damage any systems.

Qui-Gon took over the manual controls. He pushed the speed to maximum.

"That was close," Adi said.

They had escaped. But where were they headed?

CHAPTER 12

With the ship in hyperspace, Obi-Wan and Siri were able to relax for the first time in days. Taly fell asleep curled up on a cushion in the cockpit. He was exhausted.

"At least the bounty hunter has a well-stocked galley," Siri said in a low voice. "When Taly wakes up he can have a decent meal."

"We should get some rest, too," Obi-Wan said.

Siri went over to sit next to him on the cushioned seat in the cockpit. She hugged herself for a minute, hands on her elbows in an uncharacteristically nervous gesture.

"Obi-Wan? I just want to say thanks."

"Thanks for what?" Obi-Wan asked.

"I could have put Magus on our tail by selling my crystal. He might not have known for sure we were alive. Or that we were close to Settlement Five."

"We don't know that."

"I feel it. And I shouldn't have done it. But thanks for not telling me that."

"I admire you for what you did," Obi-Wan said. "Taly needed to know that you'd take care of him. He was losing hope, and I didn't see it. You did. It would be logical for

Magus to go to Settlement Five to watch the boarding of the freighter. Even if he hadn't found the vendor, he would have been there."

Siri's gaze was warm and amused. "You're a terrible liar, Obi-Wan Kenobi. It's one reason I like you so much."

"Ah, so you like me," Obi-Wan said lightly. "I thought I'd lost your good opinion."

She leaned against him for a moment, nudging him, then swung away. "Don't worry so much."

Siri's smile was so free of tension that it transformed her face. It was almost as though he had a glimpse of another Siri, a Siri without the engine that drove her, the need to excel, the stubbornness, the discipline. There was a Siri inside that Siri, someone he didn't know very well at all.

Obi-Wan felt his cheeks heat up. He looked down at his hand, resting next to hers on the cushion. He knew the shape of her fingers, the texture of her skin almost as well as his own. He had to fight the urge to slip his hand over hers, wind his fingers around hers.

Obi-Wan stood quickly. He turned his head away to hide his flaming cheeks.

Siri stretched out on the cushioned bench. She grabbed a blanket and drew it over her. She closed her eyes. He could tell she wasn't sleeping. Had he hurt her feelings by getting up so abruptly?

Obi-Wan had never worried about things like that before with Siri. Why was he so conscious of it now? Why was he so conscious of her?

He didn't like the feeling. But he liked it, too. Thoroughly confused, Obi-Wan stamped over to stare with unseeing eyes at the nav computer and try not to look at his friend again.

A day later, they drew close to the coordinates for reversion. They were almost to Coruscant.

"By nightfall, we'll be sitting in the Temple," Obi-Wan said with satisfaction. He would be glad to be back. Glad to get Taly to safety. Glad to put this mission behind him.

Siri worked at the nav computer. "Coordinates set for reversion outside Coruscant airspace."

Obi-Wan began to flip switches. He frowned.

"Everything okay?"

"I'm getting a funny readout from one of the security system checks. I've never seen one like it before."

Obi-Wan went to the manual security scan. He ran through the readouts. Suddenly, he felt the blood drain from his face.

Taly drew closer behind him. Siri spun around in her chair. "What is it?"

Obi-Wan's throat felt tight. "It's an anti-thievery device. Magus did have a surprise for us. The ship is programmed to self-destruct upon reversion." He turned to Siri and Taly. "We can't get out of hyperspace without blowing up."

CHAPTER 13

Obi-Wan looked at Siri. "How much fuel do we have?"

Siri hesitated. She glanced at Taly.

"Say it," Taly said. "I need to know, too."

"Two hours. We barely had enough to get to Coruscant."

"Cancel reversion," Obi-Wan said. "We have to dismantle this device."

"Let me look," Taly said eagerly. Obi-Wan motioned him over and pointed to the schematic on the datascreen. "There are two places to try to dismantle it — at the switch, or at the source. The only problem is . . ."

"If you do something wrong, you destroy the ship," Taly said, nodding.

Siri leaned over the datascreen. When she turned to speak, her face was very close to Obi-Wan's. She quickly moved away. "These kinds of things aren't my strong suit," she said. "I don't know engines like you do, Obi-Wan."

Obi-Wan didn't know them that well, either, but he decided it was better not to say that. He, like any Jedi, could diagnose problems, even if the shipboard computer wasn't functioning. He knew how to bypass systems and tinker with a sublight engine. But this was way over his head.

"I can try to find the contact point for the device," he said. "If only we could contact the Temple and someone could talk me through it!"

But there was no comm service in hyperspace.

"We can send a distress signal to the Temple," Siri said. "We should at least do that, so they know we're in trouble."

Even if they can't help us. Obi-Wan knew exactly what Siri would not say.

She leaned over and sent the distress signal.

Taly was flipping through diagrams on the screen. "Let me study this schematic for awhile."

Taly leaned closer to concentrate. They watched as he studied diagrams and readouts. Then he turned around. "Uh, guys? Would you mind not hovering? It's not helping my concentration."

Obi-Wan crossed to another datascreen. He and Siri went over the same information as Taly.

"I don't know what to do," Obi-Wan confided to her. "I could go over this information a thousand times, and I don't think I could figure it out."

"You'll think of something," Siri said. "Or I will, or Taly will."

"We have two hours," Obi-Wan said.

*   *   *

Time seemed to creep, but suddenly, an hour had passed. Obi-Wan tried not to look at the chrono on the instrument panel, but the seconds ticked by in his head. Taly had his head in his hands.

"There's one thing we can try," Taly finally said. "Disrupt the reversion process during the last cycle and reverse it. Then go forward again, but this time, switch over to auxiliary power. "

"In other words, you'd activate the explosion, then cancel it, and hope it doesn't reactivate in time," Obi-Wan said.

"But we have no way of knowing how fast it will re-arm," Siri pointed out. "We could blow ourselves up."

"That's the danger," Taly conceded.

Obi-Wan and Siri exchanged a glance.

"At least Taly's plan gives us a chance," Obi-Wan said.

Taly balled up his hands into fists. "I should be able to figure this out! I should be able to dismantle it!"

Obi-Wan put his hand on his shoulder. "Taly, it's all right. It's very ingenious. Very detailed. None of us can dismantle it."

"Let's wait until the last possible minute, to be sure we can't come up with another idea. Then we can follow through," Siri proposed. "Agreed?"

"Agreed," Obi-Wan said.

Taly nodded, his face pale.

It was a gamble they could pay for with their lives, and they knew it.

*　　*　　*

They had nothing left to try.

Taly sat in the far side of the cockpit. He had accessed the holomap and was simply flicking through space quadrants, one after the other, staring at the light pulses that indicated planets and moons.

Siri had disappeared from the cockpit. She had been staring at the datascreen. She had climbed down into the engine bay. She had gone over operations manuals. She had not come up with anything. Obi-Wan knew she felt just as helpless as he did. They weren't used to feeling this way.

He went searching for her. She was curled up in the cargo hold, on the floor, wrapped in a blanket. Without a word she opened the blanket so Obi-Wan could slide next to her. It was cold. He was reminded of the early morning hours they spent in the cave, watching the sun come up.

"I think we've hit something we can't solve," Siri said. "That's not supposed to happen."

"Yoda would say that Jedi aren't infallible. We are only well prepared."

"Well prepared, we are," Siri said gently in Yoda-speak. "Infallible, we are not."

They laughed softly.

"When the moment comes, we'll be together," Obi-Wan said.

He put out his hand. Siri slipped hers into it. At her touch, something moved between them, a current that felt alive.

At last he felt what it was like to touch her. He realized that he'd been thinking about it for days. Maybe for years. She wound her fingers around his, strong but gentle, just as he knew she would. He could feel the ridge of callus on her palm from lightsaber training, but the skin on her fingers was soft. Softness and strength. He'd known he would feel that.

Something broke free inside him. He felt filled up with his feeling, even though he couldn't name it. He couldn't dare to name it. Yet it was suddenly more real than anything in his life. More real than the danger they were in. More real than the Jedi.

"Siri . . ."

Her voice was a whisper. "I feel it, too."

She turned her face to his. Her eyes were brimming with tears. She half-laughed, half-cried. "Isn't this funny? Isn't this the strangest thing?"

"No," Obi-Wan said. "This has always been there. I just never wanted to see it. Since that first time I spoke to you, when you were so angry at me for leaving the Jedi," Obi-Wan said. "You were eating a piece of fruit. You just kept chewing and staring at me, as though I didn't matter."

Siri laughed. "I remember. I was out to get you. I wanted to make you angry."

"You made me furious. You always knew how to do that."

"I know. And you were always so *right*. So *fair*. You made me furious, too. Lots of times."

"And then we became friends."

"Good friends."

"And now," Obi-Wan said, hardly daring to breathe, "what are we?"

"On a doomed ship," Siri said. "So I guess the question is, what would we have been?"

She tightened her grip on his hand. She leaned forward, and put her lips against his cheek. She didn't kiss him. She just rested there. In that instant Obi-Wan felt something: a connection that bound him to her, no matter what. Siri. He wanted to say her name out loud. He wanted to never move from this cold floor. He wanted to touch the ends of her shimmersilk hair and breathe in the scent that came off her skin.

"Whatever happens," she whispered against his cheek, her lips warm and soft, softer than he could ever imagine, "I'll remember this."

Qui-Gon piloted the pod to the nearest landing available, a spaceport moon aptly named Haven. The bounty hunters tried a pursuit, but they weren't very determined and it was soon clear that they didn't regard the Jedi as much of a threat. They had somewhere to get to that was vastly more important. Bounty hunters were always concerned most with finishing the job and receiving their payments.

Qui-Gon and Adi sat at a table in a dingy café called The Landing Lights. They had tried to contact the Temple, but a meteor storm in the upper atmosphere at the spaceport had temporarily cut all HoloNet communication and grounded the ships. They had managed to procure a ship, a fast star cruiser with a pilot who would cheerfully do anything for the Jedi. It was fueled and ready to go. The only trouble was, they had no clue as to where they were going. If all had gone well, Obi-Wan and Siri had caught the freighter and were on their way to Coruscant with Taly. Their Padwans could even be waiting for them to be in touch.

"Well, we didn't learn much by boarding that ship," Adi said. "Was it worth it?"

"We acquired the tiniest bits of information," Qui-Gon said. "But with this last one, we might be able to put the puzzle together."

"M-T-G," Adi said. "A meeting."

"Exactly. So we can assume that all twenty targets will be present."

"Twenty planetary leaders at one meeting," Adi mused. "That could be any morning at the Senate. How can we possibly pin it down?"

"I don't think the meeting is at the Senate," Qui-Gon said. "Remember that Raptor said if he cancelled the mission, he'd head *back* to the Core? If the mission was on Coruscant, that wouldn't make sense." Qui-Gon glanced up at the display monitor overhead. "Interference is cleared. We can contact the Temple."

He reached for his comlink. "Let's find out what Jocasta Nu has to say." Qui-Gon quickly contacted her. Her crisp voice greeted him in seconds.

"Qui-Gon, it's about time you contacted the Temple." Jocasta Nu's tone never failed to make Qui-Gon feel like a disobedient student. "Are you aware that your Padawan has sent a distress signal from deep space?"

"No." Qui-Gon exchanged a worried glance with Adi. "From where?"

"It is not my job to interpret distress signals," Madame

Nu said huffily. "However, from what I understand, the signal was sent from hyperspace. We have been unable to track whatever ship it was sent from. It's not a registered ship."

"They aren't on the freighter," Qui-Gon said to Adi worriedly.

"Now, I suggest you tell me why you are contacting me."

"Adi Gallia and I are on the trail of a team of bounty hunters that are headed by a leader named Magus. They are set to assassinate twenty planetary leaders at a meeting."

"Twenty! That's rather ambitious."

"They are five very capable assassins. Do you have any background on Magus?"

"Magus . . . I know that name. One moment." Qui-Gon waited, knowing that Madame Nu was accessing her vast store of knowledge. All Jedi had access to the Archives, but Madame Nu had a gift for interpreting unrelated facts, as well as an unbelievable memory for names. Once she heard a name, she never forgot it. "Yes, Magus has done work for the Corporate Alliance in the past. Nothing illegal. But we suspect him of being a secret assassin. If you could confirm that, we could put him on the Galactic Apprehend List."

The Corporate Alliance! Of course. With the devious Passel Argente as Alliance Magistrate, the organization had changed from one that promoted good business relations to one that used trickery and intimidation to extend its power. But would they go so far as to back an assassination plot?

"I should be able to confirm that very soon. Now can you check on interplanetary meetings within the next five days?"

"Master Qui-Gon Jinn," Jocasta Nu said in her firmest voice, "are you aware how many interplanetary meetings there are every day in the galaxy? Hundreds, at least. Why, on Coruscant alone . . ."

"You can exclude Coruscant. And any planets in the Core. Let's start with any meeting that would concern the Corporate Alliance. And . . . my guess is it will take place in some sort of high-security location. Somewhere so safe that the leaders will forgo their usual security measures."

"All right, then. That helps. Somewhat." Qui-Gon could picture Madame Nu's thin-lipped frown. "Let's start with the treaty database . . . yes. Hmm. No, that wouldn't . . . perhaps . . . no. No, no, maybe? Let me try . . . wait . . . this is a possibility. Yes, yes, I think this is definitely a solid possibility. It's not an official meeting — not recorded, but we pick up things here and there. It's hard to keep a high-level meeting completely secret. Twenty planetary leaders, all heads of the largest worlds in their systems. They have various grievances against the Corporate Alliance and are considering a twenty-systemwide ban against conducting any business in the Alliance. They are trying to pressure Passel Argente, I imagine."

"He wouldn't like that," Qui-Gon said.

"No, indeed. He's a bully, and bullies can get nasty about such things. It would severely curtail the Alliance's power in a fairly large sector. Not to mention that it would send a message to other systems trying to resist Argente's strong-arm tactics that they can take action themselves. You see, the Senate has not been able to control these groups — like the Trade Association, and the Techno Union — we've been having a great deal of trouble with them lately —"

"Yes, I understand," Qui-Gon interrupted. He didn't have time for Madame Nu's summary of the bureaucratic problems of the Senate, no matter how insightful. "Where is the meeting to take place?"

"At a conference site on Rondai-Two. The Ulta Center — ultimate luxury, ultimate security. Do you need another Jedi team, Qui-Gon? I would be happy to pass along this information to Yoda, though it is not strictly within my purview to do so."

"I'll consult with Adi and be in touch. Thank you, Madame Nu."

Qui-Gon ended the conversation and turned to Adi. "Passel Argente. Even though he is a Senator, he is also a Koorivar and a leader of the Corporate Alliance, and his grudges against the Republic are plain to see. He's behind all this. He's not just a bully, he's cunning. He knows he has to stamp out resistance at the start. Has to hit it hard, to intimidate others who are thinking of crossing him. It's the way he operates."

"You don't know that for sure," Adi said.

"I feel it."

"Feelings are not proof and are inherently illogical," Adi said.

Qui-Gon turned to her. "Don't you feel it, too?"

After a slight pause, Adi inclined her head in her regal way. "I do."

While Qui-Gon was speaking, Adi had already located Rondai-2 on her datapad. Now she pushed the screen toward Qui-Gon.

"We're lucky. Two day's journey. We'll make it in time." Adi raised her troubled gaze to his. "But what about our Padawans?"

Qui-Gon looked out at the vastness of space, the clouds of stars. He felt the emptiness inside him, the yawning feeling he got when he knew Obi-Wan was in trouble and he could not get to him. For the shortest space of a moment, he thought of what it would be like to lose both Tahl and Obi-Wan, and the hugeness of that loss seemed to dwarf the vastness of what lay above him.

"There is nothing we can do. They'll have to take care of themselves."

CHAPTER 15

Taly suddenly burst into the cargo hold. "I remembered something."

Obi-Wan and Siri jumped up. "A way to fix the reversion?" Obi-Wan asked.

"No, no. I haven't figured that out. But I was just flipping through systems, and I saw this planet, Rondai-Two. You know when you feel a click in your head? I felt a click. I thought I heard the bounty hunter talking about a 'rendezvous' But he really said 'Rondai-Two.'"

"Are you sure?" Siri asked.

"I'm sure. He said 'on rendezvous,' which seemed weird, because nobody says 'on rendezvous.' He meant a planet."

"So that's where the mission is," Obi-Wan said. "But we can't get there." He started toward the cockpit. "We can do one thing. We can leave the information in the survivor box. If any part of the ship survives, the box might. And the information could get back to the Temple." He quickly accessed the box and entered the information into the datapad. "We need to put this in the escape pod."

Siri and Taly looked at him gravely. They might not survive, but they would have to hope that the information might.

"Now I just have to program the fact that the box has information," Obi-Wan said. "We just have to hope that whoever finds it will bring it to the Temple or the Senate. If it gets into the hands of pirates, it would be lost forever . . . and there's always space pirates lurking around the outskirts of Coruscant. . . ."

Obi-Wan's own words rang in his ears. "That's our answer," he said.

"What?" Taly asked.

"We can't reprogram in hyperspace. But we can send another distress signal. A general one this time, going out to all ships in the area of reversion. We would keep the signal open. That would allow whoever was tracking us to get a fix on us."

"Who is tracking us?"

"Nobody," Obi-Wan said. "Yet. But space pirates wait for distress signals. They like to prey on dying ships."

"I'm not getting this," Taly said.

Obi-Wan whirled around in his chair. "The ship will blow upon reversion. But what if we get *pulled out* of hyperspace against our will?"

"An interdiction field," Siri breathed. "If we go through one, we'll be pulled into realspace. But we'll also be sitting ducks," she pointed out. "The ship is almost out of power. If we're attacked, we won't be able to maneuver."

"At least we'll have a fighting chance," Obi-Wan said. "I'd rather meet space pirates than blow up."

Siri grinned. "Well, since you put it that way."

Taly swallowed. "If they capture me. . . ."

"We won't let that happen. We will fight to the death for you." Obi-Wan said. He thought for a moment. Taly looked scared and uncertain. But Obi-Wan knew one thing that would give him courage. He would treat him as an equal partner.

"You get a vote, Taly," he said. "If any of us says no, we won't do it. We'll keep with your original plan."

Taly bit his lip. "No, we have a better chance with your plan. Let's do it," he said in a rush. As he said it, he straightened. The color came back into his cheeks. "I'm ready."

Obi-Wan sent the distress signal and kept it on. Now events were out of their control. Obi-Wan tried not to watch the power drain. He tried not to think about what might happen. Siri came over to stand next to his chair. He stood and took his place beside her. They gripped each other's hands.

Taly moved to stand close to the windscreen, as though he could see what was ahead.

"Obi-Wan, no matter what happens," Siri murmured, "I want you to know —"

He looked into her eyes. "I already know."

The ship gave a violent shudder. They did not know if it

was the beginning of the breakdown, or if they were in the grip of the field.

"The interdiction field," Siri said as soon as she was sure. "It's sucking our power."

The ship groaned and shuddered. Stars seemed to wheel and crash as they entered realspace. The ship bumped and slammed against what felt like a wall. But it didn't explode.

The pirate ship was waiting.

Laser cannon boomed. Obi-Wan sprang forward to the controls. "I can't maneuver. We have no firepower. "

"They're going to board us," Siri said. "The escape pod?"

"They'll blast us right out of space," Obi-Wan said.

He stood. He drew his lightsaber. Siri drew hers. "Stand behind us, Taly," Obi-Wan said. "Just stay behind us. Don't try to fight."

They felt the shock of the landing craft hitting the loading bay. They heard the pounding of boots. Many, many boots. They heard the *clack clack clack* of droids. Obi-Wan glanced at Siri. He saw the same knowledge in her eyes. They didn't have to see them. They were too many.

They raced forward. Surprise was their only ally. They burst through the doors, into the thick of it — row after row of heavily armed pirates. They were a mangy group, all species, all sizes. What they had in common was weaponry and greed. Their faces were painted in bright colors, their belts hung with trophies from their many captures. He had never seen such a collection of fierce, ugly beings.

The corridor filled with smoke as small rocket fire ripped holes in the walls and thudded into the floors. Metal peeled back like durasheets.

Obi-Wan supposed that this was their warning shot, because the pirates didn't move.

A squat, powerful being walked forward. His thick black hair hung to his waist.

"What do we have here? Jedi? Ha! What luck! Do you know there's a bounty out for you?"

But he wasn't looking at Siri and Obi-Wan. He was looking at Taly.

Siri sprang forward. She was all energy, like a pulsating beam of light. The pirates fired, blasters and blaster rifles, rockets and darts. She flowed and struck and moved and rolled and leaped. Fire singed her tunic and did not slow her down. Obi-Wan felt sweat dampen his back as he struck again and again, knocking droids down, evading the pirate fire, and always, always, keeping himself between the attacking troops and Taly.

He was not tiring, not yet, but he could feel the hopelessness of the situation. Still, he had promised Taly not to surrender, and he would not.

And then, suddenly, over the thud of rockets and ping of blaster fire, he heard a scream.

"No! Take me!" Taly ran through the fire. Amazingly, he

was not hit. Coughing from the smoke, he yelled, "Take me, you cowards!"

"Taly, no!" Siri yelled.

"I can't let you die for me!" Taly called to them as a pirate swept him up and threw him back. The pirates roared as they tossed him like a toy, farther and farther back, to the end of the line. The last pirate holding Taly ran, while the others kept up a steady barrage at Siri and Obi-Wan.

Retreating, the pirates kept up the intense fire. Siri and Obi-Wan could not get to Taly. The pirates leaped onto the ship and took off into space with Taly, leaving Obi-Wan and Siri aboard a smoking, dying ship.

CHAPTER 16

"We need a landing site, and fast," Siri said. Beads of sweat matted her hair. The expression in her eyes was ferocious as she gazed out at the galaxy, as if challenging it to dare to defy her. As if space itself was obliged to hold up the dying ship.

The power was draining so fast that soon it would hit all systems. Then they would be unable to choose a course or guide it to land. They could see smoke billowing out from the port side. The attacking ship had chosen their blast sites carefully, it was clear. The escape pod bay was a mass of molten metal. Another blast on the port side had taken out all the weapons, and the ship listed to the side, constantly in danger of spinning out of control.

"Refueling stop on a satellite," Obi-Wan called out. "There's a huge spaceport there, plenty of landing platforms. Ten minutes away. Can the ship hold on for ten minutes?"

Siri gritted her teeth. "This ship is going to do what I tell it to do."

Obi-Wan sat in the copilot seat, although there really wasn't anything else he could do but watch Siri battle with the controls. Keeping the ship on course took tiny adjustments and a constant eye on the readout systems.

"Adi crash-landed on purpose," Siri said. "But this is going to be different, Obi-Wan. I might not be able to control what happens once we land."

He knew what she was telling him. They might not survive the crash.

"I understand," he said. "I trust you."

She shot him a quick look that was so full of courage he could only marvel at how strong she was.

"Coming up on the spaceport," Obi-Wan said.

The spaceport was on the edge of a red nebulae. The color was deep and seemed to pulse. To Obi-Wan's eyes, it seemed an impossible sight, a blooming flower in space. They would have to fly into the heart of its beauty.

"Here we go," Siri muttered.

And then the spaceport loomed at them, coming impossibly fast.

"I can't slow it down," Siri said, panic in her voice.

At this speed, the craft would surely disintegrate on contact with the unforgiving ground. Obi-Wan no longer felt he was diving into a flower. All poetry left his soul, and he saw duracrete and metal, hard substances that would pulverize this ship like a plaything.

"Cut the power!" he shouted to Siri.

She looked at him wildly. "But I won't have control —"

"They'll be enough left in the hydraulics for a few seconds. It will be all over by then, anyway."

She reached over and cut the power. The ship stopped careening but it was now in free fall, and they could just make out beings below running to safety. Obi-Wan saw one tall figure shaking his fist at them before racing to get out of the way.

"Here we go!" Siri screamed, using the manual controls to steer the ship away from the other cruisers and one large freighter. She had just enough power left in the hydraulics to aim the ship toward the empty section of the platform and pull it up so that it wouldn't smash nose-first into the ground.

He had time for a flash of a look, that was all, and then the ship was down, starting to skid with a terrible jolt that sent metal screaming and smoke billowing. Obi-Wan felt his jaws snap together. His body lifted through the air. He grabbed at the edge of a console on the way down but his legs flew up again and his body slammed down, wrenching the console from his grasp. He hit the ceiling, then the floor. He had never felt so helpless. He didn't know his limbs could move in so many directions at once. Pain rocketed through him. He could feel the ship sliding on its belly, scraping against the duracrete platform. He smelled fire.

Siri. Siri. Her name was like a drumbeat inside him. Through the smoke, through his own flailing limbs, he searched for her.

Jedi could make time slow down. Did that mean his death and hers would take forever?

He saw the glint of her hair through the smoke. She was slumped on the floor.

No!

He fought his way to her as the ship burned and slid. "Siri!"

He felt the pulse on her neck. It fluttered against his fingers.

He felt a surge of purpose. She was alive. He was alive. He would save them.

Somehow he managed to get out his lightsaber. With one arm around her, he dragged her across the floor of the cockpit. The ship was still skidding out of control across the ground, the friction heating the shell. The metal floor was already hot. Soon it would start to melt, to peel away. He willed his body. He reached out for the Force. This would take everything he had.

He half-crawled, half-slid across the floor. Siri began to stir. As soon as her eyes opened, she let him know by pushing him away. She never accepted help if she could do something herself. And she would will her body to obey.

He saw her wince as she reached for her lightsaber, but she joined him on the floor, crawling toward the wall of the spaceship. The ship was still out of control, but the crash had probably only been going on for three or four seconds.

He had time to do this. The ship would hold out. Obi-Wan activated his lightsaber and began to cut through the ship's wall. Siri joined him, sweat streaking through the grime on her face. It was so unbearably hot.

Coughing, they buried their lightsabers in the hot metal and it peeled back. Obi-Wan caught a glimpse of rushing sky and then he pushed Siri out, balancing on the toes of his boots. She reached a hand down for him and hauled him out with her amazing strength.

They balanced for a moment on the side of the sliding ship. They looked into each other's eyes. They gauged the speed and knew the jump would be hard. They called on the Force and leaped.

The Force helped them. They timed the leap high and wide so that they would be able to slow their descent. Still, the shock of the ground radiated up through their knees, and they rolled across the duracrete, putting as much distance between themselves and the ship as they could.

Ahead of them, the ship exploded.

They turned away from the blast, covering their heads. Molten metal rained down. Obi-Wan felt a piece sear his shoulder.

They slumped together, hardly daring to believe that they were still alive.

A tall being with arms almost to the ground came running. Obi-Wan recognized the being he'd seen shaking his fist at them. "What do you think you're doing?" the being yelled.

Siri and Obi-Wan stared at him.

"Surviving?" Siri said.

She giggled. Obi-Wan had never heard her giggle before. The relief flooded him. They were alive. They were alive. He began to laugh. They laughed and laughed, holding each other as they lay on the duracrete platform.

"Somebody's going to pay for this," the spaceport manager said, and they only laughed harder.

Obi-Wan waited for Siri in the hangar. They had separated in order to clean up. He had given the furious spaceport manager the registry number of the crashed ship, as well as Magus's name. Obi-Wan had no doubt that the spaceport manager would track him down somehow and demand payment for the damage.

Siri strode toward him, her hair wet and tucked behind her ears. "What now?" she asked as she came up.

"I found a pilot who will take us to Rondai-Two," Obi-Wan said. "She said that anybody who survived that crash deserves some help. It's a sublight cruiser. We leave in a few minutes. We could be landing by midday."

Siri nodded. "Nice to have some good news at last."

"We've got to get to Taly."

Siri's gaze clouded. "If he's still alive. Those pirates are going to turn him over to the bounty hunters for the reward."

"I feel that he's alive. We almost didn't make it ourselves."

"I know."

"But now that we have . . ."

Neither of them spoke for a moment. All around them, workers pushed through the hangar. But to Siri and Obi-Wan, it was as if no one else was there. They just looked at each other, remembering what they'd confessed on the ship. They tested it. Was it a result of circumstance, of being so close to death?

No. It was real. It was still between them.

"What do we do?" Siri asked. "What we feel . . . it's forbidden."

"But we can't just stop," Obi-Wan said. "We almost died. That could happen at any time, on any mission. I understand that. I accept it. But I won't accept going on without being together."

Siri swallowed. "What are you saying, Obi-Wan? We're Jedi. We can't be together. Attachment is not our way."

"Why?" Obi-Wan burst out. "It doesn't have to be that way. Rules can change. The Council can change the rules, they can find a way for us. We can still be Jedi and still . . . "

". . . love each other," Siri finished softly. "Let's name it. Let's not avoid saying what we know."

She reached out and touched his sleeve. "You know and I know that they won't change the rules for us. The Jedi Order doesn't work that way. The rules are there for reasons that go back thousands of years."

"All the more reason to change them," Obi-Wan said. "We could wait a few years, until we are Masters. Then we could be a team. We could go on missions together!"

Siri's eyes sparkled. "We would be such a great team." Then her gaze dimmed. "They won't allow it. And I won't let you leave the Jedi. I know what it cost you last time."

"I don't want to leave the Jedi. And I know you couldn't."

"It's everything to me," Siri said. "It's part of me. It's home." Her voice was soft. "But so are you."

"We'll just have to keep this secret." Even as he said it, Obi-Wan felt his heart fall. Keep a secret from Qui-Gon? Could he do that?

He's kept secrets from me.

But he was the Master. He had that right. Obi-Wan dismissed the thought. He knew it was born in the resentment he felt against anything that stood between him and what he wanted. It wasn't fair to blame Qui-Gon.

He could dismiss his resentment easily. What he could not dismiss was the awful feeling of concealing his heart from Qui-Gon.

"It would be hard."

Siri's gaze was cloudy. "It's the only way. Or else we decide we turn away from this."

Turn away? Obi-Wan couldn't bear it when her fingers dropped from his sleeve. In a matter of hours he had come to realize that Siri was as necessary to him as breathing. She was part of him. She was his heart and his lungs and part of what kept him standing.

He swallowed. "I can't turn away from this. I can't let you go."

Siri's eyes filled with tears, and that was the worst thing of all.

"We'll keep the secret, then? We'll see each other when we can, how we can."

Obi-Wan felt so dizzy. So full of relief at just being alive. So grateful that Siri was standing beside him. So full of joy that she loved him. But when he looked ahead, he saw deceit. Could he walk that path?

"We need to find Taly first," Siri said. "End the mission. Then we can decide what to do."

"Taly is the most important thing," Obi-Wan agreed.

Everything seemed against them, but strangely, he felt hopeful. They would find a way.

CHAPTER **17**

The pilot left Adi and Qui-Gon off at the main spaceport on Rondai-2, telling them that the Jedi were "one amazing nova of a group." He'd be happy to help them out anytime.

It was close to dawn. The sky was still dark, but was beginning to gray. Qui-Gon and Adi lost no time in hurrying to the meeting site. Their two-day journey had given them plenty of time to plan. The Ulta Center was an exclusive conference site that had been built specifically to host high-level corporate and diplomatic meetings.

The center took up a large compound in the city of Dal. On the journey Qui-Gon and Adi had done their research. The center boasted top-level security for the most private of meetings and retreats. They had their own landing platform on the roof where guests could arrive in secret. No one was allowed inside unless he or she was a guest. It was necessary to reserve rooms months in advance, and guests from different groups did not ever see each other, as there were separate wings for each meeting. Every guest had to undergo a high-level security check. There was no way that Qui-Gon and Adi could simply stroll in.

"Any ideas?" Adi asked. "We have to get in so we can

figure out the plan of attack. We don't want to advertise the fact that we're Jedi. Better if the bounty hunters don't know we tailed them here."

Qui-Gon glanced around. "That café is just opening. It's a fine morning to sit outside."

Adi looked exasperated. "Surely we have better things to do." She scanned the area for a moment. "Oh, I see. We can conduct surveillance from there. Is that your purpose?"

"It is," Qui-Gon said. "And I'm thirsty."

Adi raised an eyebrow instead of smiling, but he was used to that.

They ordered a pot of Tarine tea and sat at a table outside. The chill in the air began to lessen as the sun began to rise. The Rondais began to emerge from their homes and go off to work. They walked past, some with purpose, some enjoying the morning. Several stopped in at the café. It seemed to be a popular morning spot. Qui-Gon was glad of the company. It would conceal them more effectively. Rondai-2 was a cosmopolitan world with many visitors. No one gave them a second glance.

Everything here was mild — the weather, which never dipped to freezing; the landscape, which had no high mountains, only rolling hills; and the tempo of the cities, which was busy, but not frenzied. Everything at the conference center had been designed to conceal its high security and make it blend in with its pleasant surroundings.

A security wall curved around the conference center. The entrance was staffed with two security guards. The wall was softened by fountains that flowed invisibly from the top and splashed down in a continuous, musical stream to a long pool that served as a moat around the curving structure. Colored lights that were concealed underwater presented a constantly changing array of soft blues and violets. In front of the pool, flowering shrubs massed in the same colors, shading to deep purple and navy.

The conference center behind the wall was built in a radial design, with wings that extended from a central lobby like outflung arms. It was faced in durasteel that had been buffed to a medium blue. In sunlight, Qui-Gon thought, it would blend with the sky. It was a building that tried to make itself as invisible as it could.

Airspeeders and air taxis floated by. The pace was beginning to quicken. Still, these were the early morning workers, the ones who went to work when the sky was still dark.

"Security traps in the wall," Adi murmured. "Motion sensors at the gate. Iris scans for guests. It won't be easy to launch an attack here."

"Which is why it will be here," Qui-Gon said. "They feel safe here. And why else would Argente hire five bounty hunters? He knows that he's asking the impossible."

"So," Adi said, "how will they make the impossible possible?"

"Each bounty hunter has different skills," Qui-Gon said. "Gorm is brute force. Lunasa is the impersonator. Raptor is the efficient killer. Pilot is the best at planning getaways."

"And Magus?"

"He's the mastermind. He comes up with the plan. If we can put the pieces together, we can figure it out before it happens."

"In other words," Adi said, "we have to be masterminds, too." Suddenly she gave him a sharp look. "You're waiting for something. What?"

Qui-Gon took a sip of tea. "In hotels such as this, they pride themselves on not using droids to clean rooms or deliver food. Not even protocol droids. They only use living beings. They say it gives the service a 'living touch.' That beings can anticipate needs and make you comfortable, do things that droids can't."

"So?"

Qui-Gon shrugged. "Rooms have to be cleaned." He swirled his teacup. "Did you notice how Lunasa looked on the ship during the battle?"

"I noticed the weaponry she pointed in my direction," Adi said. "Can you get to the point?"

"Her hair was different."

The familiar line of exasperation appeared between Adi's eyebrows. "I don't pay attention to hairdos, Qui-Gon."

"When we first saw her, she was fair-haired. She wore her hair in braids. During the battle, her hair was short and dark." Qui-Gon noted Adi's impatience but willed himself not to smile. Adi did not spend much time in tune with the Living Force. "Did you notice that the natives of Rondai-Two are all dark-haired?"

Adi pressed her lips together. She knew now that Qui-Gon was leading her somewhere. Adi did not like to be led.

"Ah, here come the service workers," Qui-Gon said.

Across the avenue an air bus pulled up. A group of Rondai natives got off. They wore trim black uniforms. They headed up toward the security office. The officer yawned and waved them in.

"No security check," Adi breathed.

"They come every day. Guards get bored. They cut corners. That's what makes every security system fallible." Qui-Gon took a gulp of tea. "See anyone you know?"

Adi drew in her breath sharply. "It's her. Lunasa. She's walking right in! Let's go!"

"Wait a moment. The others will be arriving. I have a feeling the attack will come this morning."

"Qui-Gon." Adi's voice was sharp. "That cloud car. Look."

Qui-Gon glanced to where Adi indicated. Pilot and Raptor were in a speeder, cruising by. Squeezed between them was Taly. The boy didn't see them. He stared straight ahead. It was clear that he was trying not to look as terrified as he felt.

"They've got Taly," Qui-Gon said. "So where are Obi-Wan and Siri?"

Adi shook her head, her dark eyes troubled.

"Why are they keeping him alive?" she asked.

"And for how long?" Qui-Gon wondered.

18

Afraid of attracting suspicion, Qui-Gon and Adi left the café. They strolled down the street and doubled back, concealing themselves in the foyer of a building while office workers streamed past them.

"She will get the others in," Qui-Gon said. "Each of them — they've already planned it. Or else some of them are already inside. They've already been here for two days. We have no way of knowing."

"Except for Pilot and Raptor," Adi said. "And someone has to watch Taly, if they . . . if they don't kill him."

"If they were going to, they would have done so already. Pilot will watch Taly. He's responsible for the getaway. But Raptor still has to get inside. We know that for sure. He could be the last piece. When he gets in, the plan begins."

"We should notify security."

Qui-Gon shook his head. "Not yet. If the place goes on alert, it could hamper us from getting in. That is, if they even believe us. These bounty hunters are used to security officers. They'll mow them down in a flash. They won't be any help, and they'll lose their lives. I think we should do this ourselves."

Adi considered this. "Agreed." As much as Adi hated taking direction from someone else, she never let that interfere with her judgment.

She gazed over at the center, thinking. "The pool," she said. "We know that each suite of rooms has its own pool, too. They must be fed from a central source. And it must be substantial."

"Raptor," Qui-Gon said. "He has gills."

"Exactly what I was thinking."

Just then a large repulsorlift truck pulled onto the street, going fast. It veered out of its lane and crashed into a speeder bus. The driver waved his arms in frustration, blaming the speeder bus driver. They immediately picked out Pilot in disguise as the driver of the truck. The security guards in the entrance booth craned their necks.

"And there is the diversion," Qui-Gon said. "Come on."

They raced down the street and skirted the truck, not wanting to alert Pilot. Suddenly, they saw Raptor climb out of the flowering bushes and slip into the reflecting pool. He disappeared underwater.

Qui-Gon and Adi were only moments behind him. They donned their aquatabreathers as they ran and immediately slipped into the pool. The water was cold and surprisingly deep. They swam down quickly as the colors flashed, swimming through blue, then lavender. Adi nudged Qui-Gon. A shadow was moving, swimming quickly toward the wall. They followed.

The shadow disappeared. One moment he was there.

The next moment, gone. Qui-Gon swam forward, kicking his powerful legs. He came up against a blank wall.

Adi gestured at the bottom of the pool. Reflective surfaces had been set up and angled in different ways in order to deepen the effect of the colored lights. They had not seen Raptor's shadow. They had only seen his reflection. It had been impossible to tell the difference underneath the shimmering water. Qui-Gon wanted to groan aloud, but he didn't want to drop his breather.

Now they had lost a precious minute. They had to figure out the angles of reflection, and fast. The pool was too vast to search centimeter by centimeter. They didn't have the time. Adi kicked downward toward the reflectors. Qui Gon followed. He puzzled over the angles. Where was Obi-Wan when he needed him? This was exactly the type of thing that his apprentice was good at. Obi-Wan's brain was wired for logic.

But so was Adi's. She pointed and began to swim with a powerful stroke. Qui-Gon followed. Adi found an underwater conduit in a maze of smaller pipes. It was big enough to swim through. Qui-Gon saw her shadow on the wall in the same spot where Raptor had disappeared. She turned the lever and the sluice opened. She swam inside.

Qui-Gon followed. He could not use his arms to propel himself. The pipe was too small. He relied on kicking, following the movement of Adi's boots and the bubbles that streamed behind her.

The pipe spilled them out into another pool. The light

changed, and he knew the pool was partially open to the air. Adi began to swim toward the surface.

They surfaced silently. Across the pool and in front of a wide transparisteel door Raptor had already met up with Lunasa, Magus, and Gorm. All of the bounty hunters were heavily armed. Lunasa now had weapons strapped to her ankles and wrists. Gorm was wearing a weapons belt. A repeating blaster was strapped to Raptor's back. Magus wore an armorweave vest with various pockets and had two holsters strapped around his hips.

The four bounty hunters pushed through the door and split up. They still hadn't seen the Jedi, now running silently behind them. Magus headed for the roof, Lunasa down a corridor. Raptor took a second corridor and Gorm slipped through another door. Surprised, Qui-Gon and Adi stopped to consult for a moment.

"I'll take Lunasa," Adi said. Lunasa was still in sight, at the end of the corridor.

Qui-Gon had a split second to choose. Raptor. He was closest. The quicker they could take them down, the better.

There were only four. Five, if Pilot had somehow found a way inside. But Qui-Gon doubted that. He was betting that the huge truck outside was holding a cruiser in back that he could blast out and fly onto the roof. Taly, no doubt, was also in the back of the truck.

Four bounty hunters. Two for each Jedi. Not a problem. Qui-Gon told himself this, but he also knew that the Jedi were somewhat at a disadvantage. The bounty hunters had probably studied the structural plans of the conference center for weeks. If they'd done their job — and he had no doubt that they had — they would know every passageway, every utility turbolift, every duct.

And he also knew that time was against him. Even if one bounty hunter got through, he or she would be enough to wreak havoc.

Raptor saw Qui-Gon on his trail and veered off. He sent a blast of fire behind him, hoping to slow the Jedi down, but Qui-Gon did not ease his pace, deflecting the fire as he ran.

He followed Raptor into a vast space full of steaming pipes — the laundry. The heat and steam hit him. The clouds of vapor obscured his vision. He stopped, listening for footsteps. Only silence.

Then he heard the hiss of a rocket launcher. He was poised to move or deflect it if he could, but it hit at least a meter away.

Bad aim, he had time to think in a puzzled way, just before the pipe burst and scalding water spewed out in a violent flume.

Qui-Gon used the Force to leap and avoid the scorching water. Steam chased him as he landed meters away. Now he saw Raptor, saw his teeth flash in his grimy face as he grinned and released another rocket. As the rocket launched he charged forward toward Qui-Gon.

Qui-Gon ducked and rolled away from the rocket, which continued to chase him. Using the Force, he leaped over Raptor. Unable to track him, the rocket exploded into a large washing unit. Water sprayed out and hoses sprang from the machine like deadly snakes.

Qui-Gon backed up and collided with a bin of sheets that had been jarred from a conveyor belt. The folded sheets flew into the air like large, clumsy birds and then fell, an obstacle course of soft, downy fabric.

He saw that he had landed near a series of raised conveyor belts that ran high above his head. On the belts were large bins of linens, sheets, and towels. In a glance he saw that after being folded by droids, the sheets were loaded and sent to be dumped into bins. Then the bins continued on the conveyor belt to the exit, where wheels snapped down.

Raptor was inserting another rocket into the launcher on his wrist. Qui-Gon could see from this distance that it was a Merr-Sonn K21 — powerful enough to knock a swoop from the air and turn it into melted scrap. He saw the pinpoint of light that meant its laser homing system was activated. He had no doubt it was locked on him.

He directed the Force toward the bins. The conveyor belt moved faster. The bins smacked into each other and began to fall.

As Raptor shot the rocket, the bins crashed into it and the sheets wrapped around it, immediately interfering with its homing device. As Qui-Gon expected, the rocket slowed, momentarily hampered from target lockdown. At the same time, Raptor jumped forward in the same fashion he had moved when shooting off the other rockets. He plowed right into the sheet-wrapped rocket, which, misreading him as a target, exploded on impact. Qui-Gon turned away from the blast. Raptor was no longer a danger to anyone.

Qui-Gon now raced in the opposite direction, back toward the door through which he'd entered. He didn't want to get lost in the maze of corridors. He needed to backtrack.

He ran down the corridor and saw Adi racing toward him. "I've got Lunasa pinned down by security guards," she said. "No weapons on her. But I can't find the others. There's a security alert on, but it's silent. They don't want the guests upset."

"There'll be quite a few upset guests if we don't get Gorm and Magus," Qui-Gon pointed out. "We've got to comb this entire wing. Have you found out where the meeting is?"

"Down this way — the Constellation Suite. They're sending security there. They told me they'll handle this."

"Let's go," Qui-Gon said.

Their route took them past the place where Lunasa was supposed to be held. Four dead security guards lay on the ground.

"I shouldn't have left them," Adi said.

"You had to. Come on." Qui-Gon raced on. He was worried now. They could have used Obi-Wan and Siri in this situation. The bounty hunters were spread out. They wouldn't leave until they did their job. They would have to come together eventually, but in the meantime, anyone who got in their way would be killed.

They found the Constellation Suite. A trio of guards stood outside the doors.

"Nobody gets in," the leader of them said. "And nobody gets out. We're in lockdown."

"They'll get in somehow," Qui-Gon said. "You have to let us examine the suite."

"We've got it covered," the guard repeated frostily.

"Listen," Adi said, "you've got four dead friends down the hall. You might want to allow us to help you."

"Something wrong with your hearing? We've got it — "

Suddenly, his eyes glazed, and he fell over. Qui-Gon bent over him and saw the dart in his neck. He twisted and saw that Adi was already running.

"Magus!" she told Qui-Gon.

The remaining guards looked resolute, holding their blasters forward but occasionally glancing down nervously at their fallen comrade. Trusting that they would not fire at him, Qui-Gon barreled through and used his lightsaber to create a hole in the locked door big enough for him to leap through.

Twenty planetary leaders sat at a large meeting table. Apprehension turned to panic when they saw Qui-Gon jump in, his lightsaber blazing.

"I'm here to help," he said.

Boots thudded against the window. Lunasa had used a liquid cable to rappel down. In the same quick movement she cut the transparisteel with one hand and tossed in a grenade with the other.

"Down!" Qui-Gon shouted.

The blast rocked the room. Qui-Gon pulled as many as he could with him under the table as debris rained down. One leader was wounded. Another lay still. Qui-Gon didn't wait for the dust to clear. He leaped for Lunasa, who was reaching for a repeating rifle on her back. He slammed into her, knocking her straight out the window. Both of them flew through the air, down ten stories, and landed with a splash in the pool.

Choking, Lunasa surfaced. She tried to swim away, but Qui-Gon caught her by the legs, flipped her over, and dragged her from the water. She lay gasping on the duracrete while security officers ran toward them.

"Don't let her move," Qui-Gon told them. "Not even a centimeter."

He saw Adi on the roof. Magus was using a repeating blaster, a powerful weapon that even a lightsaber had trouble deflecting. Qui-Gon raced toward the wall. Where was Gorm? Once again he wished for the Padawans.

He deployed his liquid cable and heard it whistle as it drew him at top speed up to the roof. Once there, Qui-Gon charged toward Magus, lightsaber swinging.

Magus surprised him. He didn't continue the attack. He ran.

Qui-Gon and Adi leaped, whirling in midair as Magus

changed course and dived off the roof. He landed on a roof several stories down and smashed through a skylight.

They had left the planetary leaders unprotected, and Gorm was still on the loose. But Magus was so close. What to do? Adi and Qui-Gon landed lightly on the roof and exchanged a quick glance.

"We've got him!"

Obi-Wan yelled the words from below as he appeared, streaking across the roof with Siri. They jumped into the broken skylight, lightsabers held aloft.

Without another word, Qui-Gon and Adi activated their launchers and slid down to the meeting room. The leaders had upended the table and were crouching behind it as flames roared in from the hallway. Gorm was using a flamethrower.

The heat was intense. Qui-Gon felt it scorch his skin. The table burst into flame and the leaders scrambled backward. Gorm flipped the flamethrower back in its holster and advanced, firing. Qui-Gon and Adi leaped in front of the smoldering table. Their lightsabers were a blur of light and movement. They drove Gorm back. Half-being, half-mechanical, he was more solid than most. Although his armor had blackened from the fire, nothing had slowed him down.

Qui-Gon wanted to end this. The beings behind him were terrified for their lives, and he intended both to protect them and to make this ordeal shorter. Jedi did not fight with anger, but bounty hunters always annoyed Qui-Gon. To kill was despicable. To kill for money was worse. He did not understand the mentality of a being who would hire himself out to hurt beings. Even ten-year-old boys.

He pressed forward. Gorm's disadvantage was his belief in his own invincibility. He thought he was a fortress. He thought he was unbeatable.

Until now, Qui-Gon told him silently. *Until now.*

Gorm's plated armor was formidable, but he hadn't yet met a lightsaber. Qui-Gon moved to one side. Gorm followed. He raised his arm to come down on Qui-Gon, believing, no doubt, that he would be faster and stronger. Qui-Gon ducked so that he received only a glancing blow. It was enough to turn his knees to water, but he'd expected that, planned for it. With an upward thrust, he aimed for Gorm's helmet.

His helmet was where his intelligence was. Where his targeting system spoke to his servomotors, where his motivator powered the blasters built into his hands.

Gorm shook his head. Smoke rose from one side of his helmet. He charged at Qui-Gon again. Sensing what Qui-Gon was up to, Adi moved to the other side. Together they delivered simultaneous blows to his helmet.

The helmet melted and fused to Gorm's neck.

For a moment, Gorm looked surprised. Then his eyes turned red with fury. With a scream, he flailed at Qui-Gon and tried to pummel Adi. But the lightsabers had done their work. Signals conflicted. Servomotors malfunctioned. Gorm toppled over.

Qui-Gon bent over him. He was not dead, but he was certainly incapacitated.

Qui-Gon looked up. Magus stood stock-still at the end of the hall. With one quick glance he took in the Jedi and the monster of a bounty hunter down on the floor. He looked right into Qui-Gon's eyes and shrugged, as if to say, *Oh, well, this didn't work out too well. Time to go.*

He leaped into the turbolift.

Obi-Wan and Siri rounded the corner, frustration on their faces. "We lost him."

"The roof," Qui-Gon said.

They used their cable launchers. When they jumped onto the roof, they saw that Pilot had landed a small cruiser. Magus started to run for it. They could see Taly in the front seat.

Magus stopped and pointed his blaster at Taly's head. The Jedi stopped.

The bounty hunter's eyes stayed amused.

"You want the boy, presumably," he said.

"You know we do," Qui-Gon replied.

"Pilot, bring him out," Magus said.

"He knows our names, our faces!" Pilot yelled.

"So do they, idiot. Do it."

Grumbling, Pilot picked up Taly, who was bound hand and foot.

"Pilot will throw him off the roof if you don't allow us to get away," Magus said calmly.

Pilot balanced on the front of the airspeeder. Taly looked out at them. He had been brave for so long. Now his terror touched Qui-Gon's heart.

"You can go," he said to Magus.

But instead of waiting for Pilot, Magus leaped into the speeder. He pushed the power. With a scream, Pilot went flying, dropping Taly. Siri took a leap straight off the roof and caught Taly with her legs. They bounced at the end of her cable launcher, which she had somehow managed to hook onto the roofline even as she fell.

Pilot fell off the roof. They heard his dying scream, and then a muffled thud.

And Magus flew off, free.

CHAPTER 19

Two planetary leaders had been badly wounded, but all of them survived. Raptor and Pilot were dead. Gorm and Lunasa were taken into custody. It was good to know that the galaxy would be rid of them for a good while.

Taly was being seen to by a medic droid. The boy had a few bruises but otherwise had not been harmed. Qui-Gon squatted next to him as the medic applied bacta to a scratch on his leg.

"How did you manage it?" the Jedi asked. "How did you stay alive?"

Taly grinned, then winced as the medic droid cleaned another scratch. "I told them I'd made another copy of the conversation I'd overheard. And I knew who had hired them, and it was on the recording rod, but it was hidden in a place where if anything happened to me it would be sent directly to the Senate. They were more afraid of the being who hired them, it turned out. Someone powerful who would ruin them, or maybe even hire other bounty hunters to track them down and kill them. They had too much else to do to try to make me tell them. I think they were going to deal with me after the attack. But I knew you Jedi would show up."

"And do you know who hired the bounty hunters?" Qui-Gon asked.

"I'm not sure. There were so many things said, I was confused."

"I don't think so. I think if you heard who hired them, you would remember it exactly."

Taly said nothing. Qui-Gon realized that Taly wouldn't tell him. He might not even tell the Senate. Too much of a burden was on this boy, but he had learned in a short time how to fight. He had been given a lesson in knowledge as power, and he could be holding the most important piece of the puzzle. He wouldn't give that up.

"I would tell the Senate, if I were you," Qui-Gon advised. "Knowledge is power, but it is also danger."

"I can handle the danger."

"You'll go far in life, Taly," Qui-Gon said. He stood with a sigh.

"When can we leave for Coruscant?"

"Soon. The hotel owner is sending his own cruiser to take us back. Should be pretty posh."

Taly brightened. "And my parents? Can we see if we can contact them?"

"Yes. We'll do that, too."

Qui-Gon turned. Obi-Wan and Siri were standing alone by the pool. An alarm sounded in him softly. Something was different.

They were looking at each other. They were not joking, or fussing with their utility belts. They were simply talking.

Qui-Gon felt a quiet dread. There was something between them. Something had happened. He saw Obi-Wan smile and reach up to touch Siri's lip where a small wound was. He had seen all of Obi-Wan's smiles, and he had never seen this one before.

"We have no proof," Adi said, coming up next to him.

Qui-Gon was confused for a moment. Had Adi seen what he had seen?

"Nothing on Passel Argente. He'll get away with this. The bounty hunters won't talk, of course. We can suspect the Corporate Alliance, but I don't think we'll be able to prove it." Adi sighed. She saw the same scene he did, two Padawans standing by a pool, but she didn't notice a thing. "So it's a small victory."

"Twenty beings are alive," Qui-Gon said. "Twenty worlds didn't lose their leaders. Twenty families didn't lose their loved ones. I wouldn't call that a small victory."

Adi lifted both eyebrows at him this time to indicate just how displeased she was. "I am not diminishing that, Qui-Gon. I am just saying . . . oh, I don't know," Adi burst out with uncharacteristic emotion. "It seems that these days, we complete a mission, and we are successful, yet there is always something we could not seem to do. We get the small thing, but not the big thing. Oh, I hate being imprecise!"

"I know," Qui-Gon said. "Many of us feel this. The Senate is becoming more fractured every day. Groups like the Corporate Alliance are becoming more bold in their trickery. I have visions of a day when we are no longer peacekeepers, but warriors."

Adi looked troubled. "Visions come and go."

"This one remains."

"I hope you are wrong."

"No more than I do." Qui-Gon's gaze rested on Obi-Wan and Siri. "No more than I do."

Taly's eyes grew huge as the Senate buildings came into view. "I knew it was supposed to be big. But this . . . it's beautiful. And how can you get anywhere in these space lanes? Everything is so crowded."

"You learn your way around," Obi-Wan said. "Here's the landing platform."

The pilot guided the cruiser to a smooth landing. Taly looked back with regret at the luxurious interior of the ship. "This is probably the most amazing ship I'll ever ride on."

"Somehow I doubt that," Qui-Gon said.

They personally escorted Taly to the meeting with the Senate committee. They watched him walk inside. He hid his nervousness well.

"I hope he tells everything he knows," Adi said.

With a glance at Obi-Wan, Qui-Gon said, "No one tells everything they know."

*　　*　　*

Back at the Temple, the Jedi split up to return to their quarters to rest. Qui-Gon beckoned to Obi-Wan.

"Let's take a walk," he said. He saw the puzzlement on Obi-Wan's face. A walk after a hard mission and no sleep for three days? Obi-Wan's exhaustion was evident, but he turned without a word and fell into step beside Qui-Gon.

Qui-Gon led him to the Room of the Thousand Fountains, the place where they had always had their most significant talks. The cooling spray revived them as they walked silently along the twisting paths.

"A hard mission for you," he said. "You must have thought the worst when you were aboard that ship."

"We did not expect to survive," Obi-Wan admitted.

"And how did that make you feel?"

Obi-Wan shook his head. "It made me feel many things. Fear, of course. And regret."

"Regret?"

"Regret for things not yet done," Obi-Wan said. "Regret for not recognizing earlier . . . not being able to have . . ." He struggled and fell silent.

"Siri," Qui-Gon said.

Obi-Wan stopped. "You know?"

"I saw it between you." Qui-Gon began to walk again, and Obi-Wan moved next to him. "It happens sometimes, between Padawans. Especially during extreme situations —"

117

Obi-Wan stopped again, and Qui-Gon saw that he was angry.

"Don't," the apprentice said. "I realize what I am about to hear from you. But don't diminish it."

He spoke like a man. *He* is *a man, you fool,* Qui-Gon told himself. *And he is right. Who are you to reduce his love?*

"I'm sorry, Obi-Wan," Qui-Gon said. "Come, let's keep walking. So, you know what I'm going to say, do you?"

"That attachment is forbidden. That I have chosen this path, and I must walk it. That there is no place for such personal commitment in the Jedi Order. That each of us must be free of personal attachment or we cannot do the work we are meant to do. That a Force connection is a gift that we must honor not only in our hearts, but in our choices."

"You say these things as if they have no meaning."

"Sometimes everything falls away when you realize that you love."

And what could Qui-Gon respond to that except to say *I know*?

"We have been together for many years, Padawan," Qui-Gon said instead. "I think we have earned each other's trust and respect. It wounds me that you don't want my advice on such an important matter."

There was a struggle on Obi-Wan's face. "I don't want your advice because it will break my heart not to follow it," he said finally.

"So you will not ask for it."

"Of course I want to hear what you think, Master,"

Obi-Wan said finally. "I don't want to wound you. Yet it seems inevitable that someone will get hurt."

"Ah," Qui-Gon said. "And there is your first lesson on why love is forbidden between the Jedi."

Obi-Wan said nothing. There was just the whisper of footsteps and the soft calming splash of the fountains.

"I advise you to give her up," Qui-Gon said as gently as he could. "This is based not so much on the rules of the Jedi, but from what I know of you. Of both of you. Obi-Wan, you are a gifted Jedi. The path is one that is ingrained on your heart. On your character. If you give it up, something in you would die. I feel the same about Siri."

"But I won't give up the Jedi," Obi-Wan insisted. "The Order could change its rules."

"Know this, Padawan," Qui-Gon said. "The Jedi Council will not change the rules."

"But —"

"They will not change the precepts. Not unless the whole galaxy changes, the whole Order changes, not unless an upheaval happens that changes everything. Then, perhaps, the rules will change. But with this Jedi Council? No. Make your choice. But do it with your eyes open."

"You are asking me to tear my heart in two."

"Yes," Qui-Gon said wearily. "I am. My advice is based on this — I feel that for both you and Siri, the heartbreak of losing each other will lessen over time. You will not forget it, it will be a part of you forever, but it will lessen.

Whereas if you leave the Jedi Order, that regret will never lessen. It will always be between you and part of you. Between the two, losing each other — something that seems so terrible, so painful — will be, in the end, easier to bear."

"I can't do it." Obi-Wan looked at Qui-Gon, his gaze tortured. "Don't make me do it."

"I can't make you do anything, my Padawan. You must choose. You must talk to Yoda."

Obi-Wan looked startled. "Yoda?"

"I contacted him about this. I had to. He will keep it to himself. He has always been, next to me, your closest advisor, Obi-Wan. He is seeing you, not as a member of the Council, but as your advisor and friend. And if you cannot face him," Qui-Gon added lightly, "then you are not ready to face the Council."

They turned a corner, and Yoda sat waiting, leaning on his stick, in the middle of the path.

At the sight of him something inside Obi-Wan seemed to break. Qui-Gon saw it. Yoda did not have to say a word. Yet within this small creature was all the nobility and wisdom that Obi-Wan aspired to. Here was the best that the Jedi path could lead to.

"Sacrifice, the Jedi Order demands," Yoda said. "No reward for you in it, either, Obi-Wan. Support you, we will. Change the rules for you, we will not."

Obi-Wan sank heavily down on a bench. He put his face in his hands. Qui-Gon saw his shoulders shake.

He did not think it was possible for his heart to break any more than it was broken already. Yet this must be it, the worst thing for him to have to bear. To give to the boy he loved like a son the same pain he felt. To hand it over, knowing what it would do to his heart.

It took a long time for Obi-Wan to regain mastery over himself. Qui-Gon and Yoda waited silently. At last Obi-Wan raised his face to them both. "What about you?" he said quietly to Qui-Gon.

Qui-Gon started. He knew, of course, what Obi-Wan was referring to. Tahl. He did not expect to be challenged about it. He did not expect to have to talk about it.

Yet, why not? Obi-Wan had every right to raise the question.

"You loved Tahl," Obi-Wan said. "You broke the rule. And now you're asking me to give up something that you took for yourself. What were you and Tahl thinking when you pledged your love?"

"Yes, Qui-Gon," Yoda said. "Interested I am in your answer as well."

Qui-Gon thought before he replied. He did not want to answer this question. It touched on the deepest part of him. If he spoke her name aloud, would he crack?

"It was a confused time," he said. "We barely had time to acknowledge what we felt before she was kidnapped."

"An answer, that is not," Yoda said.

"What were we thinking?" Qui-Gon passed a hand over his forehead. "That we would find a way. That we were

Jedi, and we would be apart much of the time. Yet we wouldn't deny the feeling."

"You would break the rule," Obi-Wan said. "You would have kept it secret."

Qui-Gon shook his head. "No, I don't think either of us wanted that. I think we felt that we would work something out somehow."

"The same way I feel now!" Obi-Wan cried.

Qui-Gon sat next to him on the bench. "Here is the difference between us. I did not get a chance to examine my decision. To see its pitfalls and its faults. I do not know what would have happened if Tahl had lived. We might have decided to put our great love aside. We might have left the Jedi Order. I do not know. I will never know. And I live with the heartbreak of losing her. But I am living, Obi-Wan. I am continuing to walk the Jedi path. What I'm saying to you is that once in a great while we have a chance to look at our lives and make a choice that will define us. You have that choice. It is ahead of you. Do not make it in haste. Use your head as well as your heart. Remember that you have chosen a life that includes personal sacrifice. This is the greatest sacrifice you can give."

"Add only this, I will," Yoda said. "Feel some of us do that great troubles lie ahead. We cannot see them or know them, but feel we do they are waiting. Need you, we do, Obi-Wan."

"And how will you feel," Qui-Gon said, "if the great troubles come, and you are not standing with us?"

"I don't know what's right." The words seemed torn from Obi-Wan. "I don't know what to do!"

Siri appeared at the top of the path. She ran toward them, her face stricken with sorrow.

"Magus has struck," she said. "Taly's parents have been killed."

CHAPTER 20

"Revenge," Qui-Gon said heavily. "It creates the greatest evil."

Yoda rose. "We must see what we can do for Taly."

"He gave information to the committee on the bounty hunters, but he did not reveal if he knew who had hired them," Siri told them.

"We'll never know the answer," Qui-Gon said.

"Increasing in power, the dark side is," Yoda said. He looked at Obi-Wan and Siri.

Qui-Gon and Yoda walked away. Siri stared after them.

"It's almost as if Yoda knows about us," she said.

"He does."

Obi-Wan drank in the sight of her. Her crisp beauty, the way she stood and moved and talked. The compassion in her eyes for Taly. He had come so close to having her in his life, to sharing things with her that she would not share with anyone else. So close to knowing her best. Loving her best.

"Don't look at me like that," Siri said, almost in a whisper. "You look as though you're saying good-bye."

Obi-Wan said nothing.

Her hand flew to her mouth. "What did they say to you?"

"They said to me what I already knew. What you already know. The rules will not change. And if we leave the Jedi together, we will never rest easy with that decision. We will regret it every day. And sooner or later that would lie between us and be greater than our love."

She turned away angrily. "I don't want to look that far ahead. I don't believe you can see what will happen. Anything can happen!"

"So what do you want to do?" He touched her shoulder. At first she jerked away, but then she relented. She leaned against him, her back against his chest. He slipped his arms around her waist. He couldn't help himself. *I will give you up, Siri. But not yet. Give me this last moment, Qui-Gon. Let me brush my mouth against her neck. Let me feel her shudder.*

"I didn't want to decide," Siri said. "Isn't that weak of me? I wanted you to decide. I was so afraid of what lay ahead that I wanted to let go of my own will." She shook her head, and he felt her hair swing against his cheek. "Is this what love is? Then maybe I'm not cut out for it after all."

He smiled at her rueful tone, even though his heart was breaking. He tried to turn her to face him, but she resisted.

"No. I can't look at you right now. Just . . . don't move." Her voice was a murmur now, and he could hear the tears behind it.

"I know we have to let each other go," she said slowly. "I can't imagine walking out of this room without being together, but I know it has to be done."

"You know that the Jedi need our service," Obi-Wan said.

Siri sighed. "Oh, Obi-Wan. Try not to be pompous." She twisted in his arms, ready to face him now, mischief in her eyes. "That is a trait I would tease out of you, given the chance."

"I'm sure you would. And I would tease your impatience with rules out of you."

"Yes, you were always better than me at the acceptance part."

Her words sank in, and the light left her eyes. "Even now," she said. "Even now you're teaching me acceptance, just at the moment I don't want to hear about it."

"Siri —"

"Wait." She pulled away from him and backed up. "Here is another thing you know about me — I don't like to drag things out. So let's make a pact. There's only one way this is going to work. We have to forget it ever happened."

"Forget?" Obi-Wan looked at her, incredulous. "I can't forget!"

"Well, you just have to," Siri insisted. "You have to push it down. You have to bury it. I'm not saying it's going to be easy. But I am going to do it. I am not going to think of you or wonder if we did the right thing. There will be no special looks exchanged when we see each other. You will never mention what happened between us again. We will be comrades when we meet. Comrades only. I am *not* going to look back, not once." She stamped her foot, as if stamping the memory into the ground. Obi-Wan started at the sound, wincing as though she had struck him. She was a warrior now, willing her body and mind and heart to obey her.

"And you will never remind me," she continued. "Not by a word or a look. Promise me."

"Siri, I —"

"Promise me!"

Obi-Wan swallowed. "I promise."

Her face softened for an instant. The last instant, he suddenly knew, he would see her look at him that way. "And I hope," she said, a catch in her voice, "that we don't meet for a long, long time."

Now that the moment was here, Obi-Wan saw more clearly what was ahead. A chasm of longing inside him that he would not be able to ever, ever fill up. A loss he could never acknowledge.

I can't do it, he thought, taking a step toward her. He had to touch her one more time. Maybe that would change everything.

"No." She backed up. "It starts now. May the Force be with you."

She turned and ran down the path. He reached out blindly for her. He felt the empty space where she'd stood. The waterfalls continued to mist the air, and he felt the spray on his cheeks. It tasted of salt, of tears.

Part Two

Twenty Years Later

"The problem is," Mace Windu told the Jedi Council, "that Count Dooku has had years to plan the Separatist uprising. We are still catching up. We gain small victories, but they grow stronger. What we need is to strike a big blow. Something that will turn the tide and get undecided worlds to join us."

"A battle?" Anakin Skywalker asked.

"No." Mace steepled his long fingers. "Something else." He turned to Obi-Wan. "Do you remember the name Talesan Fry?"

The truth was, the name was buried. He had piled mission upon mission on top of it. When the thought of the boy crossed his mind, he thought of something else. He forgot the name of the planet Taly was from, erased the memory of the ship rigged to explode, never thought of the cave he'd slept in for close to a week.

Yet even before the full name had left Mace's lips, he had remembered every detail.

"Of course."

"Kept track of young Taly, we have," Yoda said.

"Responsibility, we had, to protect him better than we had his parents."

Obi-Wan turned to his Padawan. "Taly had agreed to testify against some bounty hunters out to attack a meeting of planetary leaders. We foiled the attack, Taly testified, but one of the bounty hunters killed his parents in revenge."

"Who was behind the attack?" Anakin asked.

"Suspect we did that it was Passel Argente," Yoda said. "Prove it, we could not."

"Taly went underground," said Ki-Adi Mundi. "Took an assumed name. But then he popped up, under his own name again. He's an adult now, of course. He spent his years underground developing his knowledge of surveillance. He's fulfilled his early promise and become the foremost expert in the galaxy. He's a leading innovator of surveillance tactics and equipment. He built an empire. He's also a recluse."

"Who can blame him for that?" Obi-Wan muttered.

"He barricades himself behind the security he developed. All his workers have to agree to live in the complex. He has several trusted associates who deal with the necessary details of his business, visiting clients and such. He has no contact with the outside. He has no friends, no family, no allegiances. His only uncle died some time ago. He's managed to stay neutral in the Clone Wars."

That sounds like Taly, Obi-Wan thought.

"Now he has contacted us. While developing new

surveillance-blocking technology, he stumbled on a startling invention." Mace leaned forward. "A foolproof codebreaker."

"Nothing is foolproof," Anakin said.

"We've seen the tests," Mace continued. "This technology could allow the Republic to break the code of the Separatists. And continue to break it no matter how many times they change it."

"Is Taly giving the codebreaker to us?" Obi-Wan asked.

Ki-Adi grimaced. "I wish it were that simple. Taly feels he owes the Jedi, because we saved his life. He's willing to offer us the technology first — if we come up with the right price. Taly has made it clear he's perfectly willing to turn around and offer it to the Separatists. What the Jedi must do is go to his compound and obtain the codebreaker, then bring it to the Azure spaceport. We've assembled a team of tech experts to study and deploy it. We know a Separatist attack is imminent. We need to discover where it will be."

"Who will go to Taly's compound?" Obi-Wan asked.

"You and Anakin," Mace said. "Taly asked for you, Obi-Wan. In consultation with Supreme Chancellor Palpatine, the Senate will send a representative as well, Senator Amidala from Naboo. She's proven to be an able negotiator for the Republic cause."

Obi-Wan noted Anakin's start. He knew Anakin and Padmé had forged a friendship. Although he liked Padmé and knew she'd be an asset on the mission, he wished the Chancellor had picked another Senator. It wouldn't do Anakin good to be around her too much.

"I have to object," Anakin said.

Mace raised his eyebrows. He was always surprised when someone disagreed with him. Beings rarely did.

"This mission could be dangerous," Anakin went on. "We already know that there have been attempts on Senator Amidala's life. We would be putting her in harm's way."

"It does not seem to me that the Senator turns away from danger if she sees a need to act," Mace said.

"And we could also be drawing the opposition. No doubt they are watching her every move."

"I have no doubt that we will be able to maintain secrecy," Mace said drily, "thank you though, Anakin, for the reminder."

"I just think there must be a better choice," Anakin said. Obi-Wan wanted to give him a hint to stop, but he didn't think it would have any effect. "Senator Bail Organa from Alderaan, for example —"

"This is the Chancellor's decision. Not the Jedi's. We cannot forbid her to go. Especially," Mace added sharply, "when we welcome her help."

If Anakin felt the sting of the rebuke, he gave no sign of it. There was no graciousness in his manner as he inclined his head, only a reluctant assent.

The passion in his Padawan's voice sounded an alarm in Obi-Wan. It stirred a memory. What had it felt like, to connect to a woman, to want to protect her?

He tamped down the memory as it rose.

I am not *going to look back, not once.*

The doors to the Council Room slid open, and Siri strode in. Since her Padawan, Ferus Olin, had left the Jedi Order years before, she had never taken another.

"I see that being at war hasn't helped your punctuality," Mace said severely.

"No," Siri admitted freely. "It's made my tardiness worse. There's so much more to do. But perhaps my excuses are improving."

Mace frowned. He didn't care for levity in the Council Room. "I have already briefed Obi-Wan and Anakin on the mission. It involves someone you may remember. Talesan Fry."

There was no reaction on Siri's face. No involuntary movement of her body. Her gaze stayed clear, her chin lifted. She did not look at Obi-Wan.

Ki-Adi Mundi went on to describe the mission. Siri listened impassively.

It was as though she had no memory of what had happened. As though she had wiped it clean.

She had buried her memories better than Obi-Wan had. He would follow her lead.

CHAPTER 22

Anakin strode along the walkway to the Senate. A speeder would have been faster, but he needed to feel the thud of his boots on the permacrete and hope the air would cool his temper. So far it grew with the pace of his walk.

He shouldn't have challenged Mace. He knew that. But he had been so stunned when Mace had told him Padmé would be on the mission that he had spoken without thinking. How could Padmé agree to this without telling him? Why would she agree at all?

Anakin thought he'd made some valid arguments, but Mace hadn't even listened, as if Anakin was still a youngling. Mace hadn't considered that he might be right, that putting a Senator in danger was a stupid idea. Their support in the Senate was crumbling by the day. Why should they risk losing such an important ally?

Of course, the reason he didn't want Padmé to go was more personal than that. She'd nearly been killed several times by an assassin. Why would she deliberately risk her safety? Anakin shook his head. He did not understand his wife. He only knew he loved her. Hungered for her. Needed her. And he could not let anything happen to her.

He had one last chance. Chancellor Palpatine had urged him to come share with any problem, no matter how small. Anakin knew that if Mace found out he'd gone around him, his momentary annoyance would change to anger, but he couldn't help himself. Palpatine was the only one who could order Padmé not to go.

The Blue Guards were standing at attention when he walked in. Sly Moore walked forward, her shadow robe moving with her gliding walk. She pressed a button on the wall. "You may go right in," she told Anakin.

Some Senators waited days or weeks until Palpatine could find a spot for them in his crammed schedule. But Palpatine had given a standing order to Sly Moore that when Anakin came, he would be seen immediately.

The Supreme Chancellor rose when Anakin hurried in.

"Something is wrong, my friend," he said, coming around the desk and approaching him with concern. "What can I do to help?"

"You know about this mission to Talesan Fry's headquarters?" Anakin asked.

"Of course. It could lead to the end of the Separatists. To peace. It is crucial."

"I understand you have picked Senator Amidala to accompany the Jedi," Anakin said. "I told Mace Windu my objections."

"Then tell them to me," Palpatine said. "I'm anxious to hear them. I always respect your opinion, Anakin. You know that. You have wisdom deeper than anyone I've ever known. You can see further than the Jedi Council."

Anakin felt uncomfortable when Palpatine said such things. But then again, there were times when he believed them himself.

"Whoever goes on this mission is in danger," he said. "Senator Amidala has survived several attempts on her life. But assassins could still be tracking her. We compromise our safety and hers if she goes. "

"All of this is true," Palpatine said. "I had not thought of those things." He clasped his hands together, his skin so pale that Anakin sometimes wondered if blood actually ran in his veins. "Anakin, I wish that I could help you. Especially in the light of your excellent argument. But I am not ordering Padmé to go. She chooses to go. How can I take back an order I did not give?"

Stopped in his tracks, Anakin didn't know what else to say. But Palpatine, as usual, had shown him the path. He needed to talk to Padmé directly. Palaptine couldn't order her not to go. But Anakin could.

Padmé's laughter bubbled, then died when she saw he was serious.

"You're *ordering* me?"

"Yes. I have a right. I have more experience than you

do; I'm a Jedi and I know what we could be in for. I'm also an officer in the Republic army."

"But I'm not." Padmé continued to fold a robe she was placing in a small bag at her feet. "So thanks but no thanks, *Commander*."

"It's dangerous and unnecessary for you to go, and I won't allow it."

Padmé turned. Her gaze was direct. Cool and composed. That always infuriated him.

"I think you know well enough how your attitude angers and upsets me. I don't respond to orders. I am a Senator. I have a duty to perform. So I am going."

"Padmé, please." He wanted to give in to her softness, but she stood before him, ramrod straight. She wasn't wearing her ceremonial robes, only a soft sheath down to her ankles, but she might as well be costumed in armor.

He collapsed on his back on the sleep couch. "I don't know why it's so hard to talk to you."

"That's because you're not talking to me. You're ordering me."

"I'm just trying to keep you safe."

"This is not the way to do it."

He looked up. She was smiling at him. She came and sat beside him.

"I know you worry about my safety," she said in the soft tone he loved. "I worry about yours. We live in perilous times, Anakin. We're in the middle of a war. I'm in danger no matter where I am. We've both been in some kind of danger since the moment you arrived to protect me."

"Agreed. But do you have to *volunteer* for it?"

She took his hand and laced her fingers through his. "I offered to go because I knew I would be safe. I knew the best Jedi in the Order would be there to protect me."

He groaned. "Now don't start flattering me."

She grinned at him. "I meant Obi-Wan."

He tossed a pillow at her, and she shrieked in surprise. She threw it back, and he held it suspended in the air with the Force.

"Are you still trying that same trick on me?"

"It's worked in the past."

She lay down beside him. They faced each other, almost nose to nose.

"I'll be careful," she said.

"I won't leave your side," he said.

"Don't," she said, drawing him close. "I don't want you to."

CHAPTER 23

The planet Genian had so far managed to remain neutral in the Clone Wars. This feat had little to do with canny diplomacy, though the Genians were indeed noted for that particular skill, but more to do with the vast corporate holdings on the planet, the research laboratories, and the treasures locked in secure banks. One day, perhaps, Genian would fall, but it was not in a terribly strategic position and at this point in the war many Senators, both Separatist and Republic alike, found it useful to be able to slip in and out to sit with their wealth and make sure it was safe.

Taly was not the only one to take advantage of friendly laws and a large, educated workforce. Many businesses thrived on Genian, primarily in the technological and scientific sector. There were a number of large, prosperous cities, but Taly had chosen to site his complex in the vast desert that lay outside the city of Bruit. Mountain ranges ringed the desert, and the countryside was rugged enough that no towns or settlements were within hundreds of kilometers.

Taly provided for his workers by supplying them with a small city, with entertainment and leisure activities and luxurious dwellings that his workers would not be able to afford in the cities. The only thing he would not allow was families. Workers had to be single and childless. He said this was because personal connections interfered with work habits, but Obi-Wan had to wonder if there was a deeper reason.

The Jedi and Padmé had traveled on a fast Republic cruiser. The journey had taken less than a day. Anakin flew low over the desert, lower than Obi-Wan would have liked, skipping over the boulders and rocks, some of them fifty or a hundred meters tall, then zooming down to hug the ground again.

"This isn't a Podracer, Anakin," Obi-Wan said.

Siri grinned and Padmé smiled.

"He does this to me on purpose," Obi-Wan grumbled.

"I don't see the landing platform," Padmé said. "I don't even see the compound."

"It's behind a holographic portal," Anakin explained. The Jedi had been thoroughly briefed on Taly's security plan. "The hologram mimics the landscape. It's hard to see."

Padmé drew closer and leaned over Anakin's shoulder. "Can you see it?"

Obi-Wan watched them, her dark head against his shoulder. They had the ease of intimacy. Long friendship, he wondered, or attraction?

"When I use the Force, I can. See the shimmer over there, by that big rock?"

A craggy rock — at least a hundred meters tall — rose over the others.

"No," Padmé said, half-laughing as she shook her head. "I just see a big rock."

In answer, Anakin flew straight toward the rock. Padmé braced herself. Obi-Wan sat calmly. He wasn't about to admonish Anakin again. Let him have his fun.

Anakin did not slow his pace. The rock loomed, closer and closer. Just at the moment of impact, they passed through it, punching a hole through the image of rock, sand, and sky.

The landing platform lay ahead, a small, circular pad outside a larger hangar. Beyond it rose Taly's compound, a series of connected buildings made of stone that matched the desert tones of ocher and sand.

Anakin guided the ship to a featherweight landing. A male of middle years stood waiting. Obi-Wan recognized the violet-tinged skin of a native Genian. The visitors grabbed their kits and headed down the ramp.

Obi-Wan announced their names, and the Genian nodded. "You are expected," he said. "I am Dellard Tranc, head of security for the complex. Please follow me."

They followed him through the hangar. Anakin whistled softly when he saw the state-of-the-art cruisers lined up in the hangar bays.

"Very nice," he murmured to Obi-Wan. "He can get anywhere in a hurry, that's for sure."

The hangar door opened into a long corridor.

"We're now in the main building," Dellard Tranc said. "I'll escort you to the main business office."

The natural stone around them was like being in a cave. It was cool and dim. Obi-Wan was used to business complexes being built of durasteel and transparisteel, as if the corporations were trying to advertise their purity by using transparent materials in their buildings. He found the natural materials here refreshing.

They entered a large office suite, and Tranc left them with a bow. Two people stood in the center, waiting for them. A trim woman about Obi-Wan's age came toward them. Her skin was lavender-colored and her hair was white. "Welcome," she said. "My name is Helina Dow. I'm Talesan Fry's executive in charge of production and distribution." She smiled briefly. "In other words, his second-in-command."

The male Genian at her side nodded at them. "And I'm Moro Y'Arano. Executive in charge of business outreach. Talesan asked me to be present at the meeting."

These were the trusted advisors Mace had spoken of, the ones who were Taly's connection to the outside. Obi-Wan introduced them all. Helina bowed. "It's an honor to meet such distinguished Jedi and officers in the Republic army. Senator Amidala, your reputation precedes you. Thank you all for coming. Please follow us."

The double doors opened into Taly's office. In contrast to the neutral colors of the walls and floor, a table made out of a golden-tinged stone served as a desk. Two tall lamps behind the desk sent out a glow with an orange-yellow tint. On one side of the office, a seating area was set up, a long, cushioned sofa and a low table made out of the same gold-hued stone.

Taly sat behind the desk, his hands clasped in front of him. Obi-Wan was surprised at the man he'd become, but he couldn't say why. He recognized the same sharp intelligence in the eyes, the thin features, the rusty shock of hair. Taly had not grown very tall or broad. He was thin, and vibrated with an intensity Obi-Wan remembered well. But there was something missing. . . .

Ah, Obi-Wan thought. The eagerness in Taly's eyes. The wish to be liked. That was gone. But of course it was. Taly was a man now, not a boy. A vastly wealthy man. Obi-Wan could not imagine the amount of grit and guile it would take to amass such a fortune, to be such a success in the cutthroat business of surveillance.

"Obi-Wan Kenobi and Siri Tachi." Taly rose and came toward them. He stood in front of them, searching their features. "You look older."

"That seems inevitable," Siri said.

For a moment, Obi-Wan felt rocked on his feet. Seeing Siri and Taly standing together had brought back a memory of a night in a cave, a thermal cape draped around two bodies, low voices, laughter. Of the cold, hard floor of a cargo hold, a coldness he did not feel.

Memories that, when they came, he always pushed down and buried.

He pushed, but the memories did not obey. They surfaced again, rising. Siri's smile. Her lips resting against his cheek.

Whatever happens, I'll remember this.

She met his eyes. He saw the memory there, reflected back. Or did he? A light went out, a shutter closed. She turned away.

"Please sit down," Helina said. Obviously, it was up to her to observe the polite rituals of meetings. "I'll ring for refreshments."

Taly led the way to the seating area. Within moments, food and drink arrived.

Taly leaned forward earnestly. "I don't pay attention to politics. I had my fill of Coruscant and the Senate a long time ago. But when I made this discovery, it was obvious how valuable it was. Politics has found me again, for the second time in my life. I am as unhappy now as I was the first time it did."

"Politics is another name for greed and corruption these days," Padmé said. "But we must not forget that it is also about compassion and justice."

Taly frowned at her for a moment as though she was speaking a language he didn't understand. "I had to choose between the two of you. The Republic and the Separatists. So I examined the two sides. The Separatists have much in their favor. They have the guilds and the trade associations. They have vast amounts of wealth and much power in the Senate. Most important, they have ruthlessness. There is nothing they won't do for power. But you — the Jedi — you tip the balance. Thousands of you are ready to fight for the Republic. I have seen what a handful of Jedi can do. I decided to bet on you. Because, believe me, I want to be on the winning side."

"Thanks," Obi-Wan said. "But we see this struggle as a noble cause, not a gamble to wager on."

Taly waved a hand. "Noble cause — sure, okay. The point is, I want you to know that if we can't come to an agreement, I'm ready to turn the codebreaker over to the Separatists. I'm giving you the first shot because I owe you, first of all, but also because I think you can win — *if* you have my device."

"We are authorized to make a deal," Padmé said. "What are your terms?"

Taly named a price. Obi-Wan sucked in his breath, but Padmé's face was impassive.

"That can be done," she said. "You would have to accept two installments, however. The first immediately, the second after the codebreaker is in our hands and has been proven to work. Do we have a deal?"

"Whoa, not so fast, Senator," Taly said. "I haven't finished. I also want an exclusive contract with the Republic. You only use Fry Industries surveillance and communication devices in the Republic army for the duration of the war."

"But that would mean abandoning systems that we already deploy and putting millions of credits into a system we don't need," Padmé said.

Taly shrugged.

Obi-Wan couldn't believe it. The brilliant, vulnerable boy he'd known had turned into a war profiteer.

"All right," Padmé said. "We will agree to this if you give us six months to make the transition. And, of course, if your system works. We have to do it gradually. I will not endanger our troops for your profit."

"Fine. I don't want anyone to get killed for me. I just want the business," Taly said. "We have a deal. Helina, can you get the contracts?"

Helina rose and departed.

"And Moro, can you bring me the model scenarios we developed for deployment of the codebreaker? We can surely share them with our new friends."

"Of course." Moro rose and left.

Obi-Wan noted how Taly watched until the door closed behind Moro and Helina. Then he activated a small device he had hidden in his palm.

"What —" Siri started, but Taly held up a finger.

He entered a code into the device, then waited for a green light.

"We have been under surveillance," he said. "Recently, I have discovered that there is a spy in my organization. Someone who wants to launch a takeover of the business. I have been able to intecept the surveillance device, but only for very short periods. I don't want him or her to know I'm onto them."

"Do you have a suspect?" Obi-Wan asked. "Is that why you sent Helina and Moro out of the room?"

"I don't suspect them any more than I do the rest of my top executives," Taly said. "Anyone who has access to my inner office. That is a handful of workers."

"Do you think the Separatists know about the code-breaker?" Padmé asked.

"All communication leaving the compound is monitored," Taly said. "That's what happens when you work for a surveillance company — I make it impossible for you to spy on me. I control all access to communication. I monitor all outgoing messages."

"Just like Quadrant Seven," Siri said.

"I learn from experience," Taly said. "So no, Senator, I don't think the information has been passed. Yet. But this brings me to my third condition for making a deal."

"We already made a deal," Padmé said.

"Not quite. You must find out who the spy is. And you must do it in the next twenty-four hours. Only then will I hand over the codebreaker."

Anakin's gaze was flinty. "The Jedi are not detectives."

Taly rose. "They are now. It is non-negotiable."

The Jedi and Padmé exchanged glances. Padmé turned back to Taly.

"We accept," she said.

CHAPTER 24

"This is ridiculous," Anakin said as soon as they were left alone in their quarters. They had already done a sweep to ensure that they were not under surveillance of any kind. "He's holding us hostage, expecting us to solve his business problems."

"True," Obi-Wan agreed.

"We're wasting time," Siri said, sounding as impatient as Anakin. "I hate wasting time. He's taking advantage of us, and he knows it."

"The codebreaker could make the difference for the Republic," Padmé reminded them. "It's vital that we obtain it. Isn't that worth a little snooping?"

Siri threw down her survival pack with an irritable gesture. It thunked against the floor. Obi-Wan gave her a curious look. He had seen Siri be impatient before — many times, as a matter of fact — but there was an edge to her mood now that he couldn't identify.

"Well, we might as well start now," Anakin said. "Taly said he'd get us a list of the executives who have access to his private office. Until then, I'm going to take a look around, get a feel for the place."

"I'll join you," Padmé said. "Maybe we can come up with something to go on."

The door hissed behind them. Siri's survival pack had snagged on the leg of a table, and when she tugged at it, some of the contents spilled out onto the floor. She gave it a swift kick for its disobedience.

Obi-Wan leaned down and gently unwound the strap of the pack from the table leg. "Are you angry at the pack, or the table? Or me?"

Siri sat on the floor and looked up at him. "I didn't think we'd have to stay here."

"Only for a day."

"A day can feel too long, if it's long enough. What do I know about corporate intrigue?" Siri growled. "I'm not the right Jedi for this job."

"You're the right Jedi for any job." Obi-Wan sat next to her on the floor. "What is it?"

"I just told you."

"No, you didn't."

She looked at him, chin first. Defensive, challenged, annoyed. Then she let out a breath, and she shook her head ruefully.

"Do you remember," she said, "in the cave, when I wanted to help him escape?"

Obi-Wan felt his breath catch. They had not talked of this in almost twenty years. The subject of the mission with Taly was too close to the reality of what had happened between them.

He kept his voice light. "One of our many arguments."

"What good did it do to have him testify?" Siri asked. "A bounty hunter alliance was smashed. Some bounty hunters went to prison worlds. I haven't kept track, but I bet some of them are free now. His parents were killed, and now look at him. Look at what that boy has turned into. This unstable, suspicious, bitter man who only cares about wealth and power. But inside, the boy is there, I feel it, and he's still in pain. Did you notice his office? The desk, the lamps? What did they remind you of?"

Obi-Wan shook his head, baffled.

"The two orange lights," Siri said softly. "The golden desk."

Obi-Wan let out a breath. "Cirrus. The two suns, the golden sea."

"He hasn't forgotten what he lost. Not for a minute," Siri said. "What if we'd let him go? What if he'd been allowed to grow up in a loving family?"

"Jedi do not deal in ifs."

Siri shook her head, exasperated. "Obi-Wan, for star's sake, you can irritate me like nobody else. Jedi don't become Generals in galactic-wide wars, either. Jedi don't watch their fellow Jedi be blown apart in great battles. Things have changed. Have you noticed?"

"Yes," Obi-Wan said quietly. "I've noticed. But I still don't believe that looking back and questioning decisions you made twenty years ago is helpful or fair."

"Once, for me, there were no questions, only answers,"

Siri said. As her mood altered, her brilliant blue eyes shifted to navy. He had forgotten how that happened, how the color of her eyes could deepen with her feelings. "I've changed. Now I question everything. I've seen too much, I fear too much of what the galaxy is becoming, " She turned her direct gaze to him. "Don't you ever look back and question what you did about something? Wonder if there was something you could have done differently?"

"That is a dangerous place for a Jedi to be," Obi-Wan said. "We do what we do, as Qui-Gon used to say."

"Qui-Gon lived in a different time," Siri said. She leaned her head back against the wall. "When Ferus was still with me, we went on a mission to Quas Killam, out in the very edge of the Mid-Rim. We were to oversee peace talks between two government factions who were trying to form a coalition. One side was a cartel that controlled much of the planet's supply of trinium, a mineral used in the man-ufacturing of weapons systems. Very important, and it made many Killams very rich. We oversaw the talks, saw a coalition government formed. A very successful mission. But Ferus said to me, *Something isn't right here. The cartel made too many concessions. It's as though they know something we don't.* And I said, *What can we do? Our mission is done. Jedi do not interfere in planetary politics. And we have many places to go.* I'm sure you've said the same to Anakin." Siri stopped. She sighed. "At the start of the Clone Wars, the Trade Fed-eration worked in alliance with the head of that cartel to take over the government of Quas Killam. Now they own all the factories, all the mines of trinium. The Killams who were not in the cartel — many of them were killed. Many of them were forced to work in the factories."

"I've heard this of Quas Killam," Obi-Wan said. "Are you saying you could have prevented it?"

"I don't know," Siri brooded. "But what if I had stayed? What if I had observed a little more closely, wondered a little more? We know the Separatists and Count Dooku plant seeds. They're willing to wait years for results. They were preparing for this, while we were going on peace missions. What if we had listened better and did more years ago, when it would have had an impact? "

Obi-Wan shook his head. "Siri, you are asking too much of yourself. Of us all."

"You didn't answer my question," Siri said.

"Question?"

"Do you look back?"

Did he look back? Of course he did, all the time. Mostly about Anakin. At a time they should be closest, they were further apart than ever. What could he have done differently? Had he turned his face away from what he did not want to see? Anakin was still his Padawan, but Obi-Wan was hardly his Master. Anakin had gone to a place where Obi-Wan could not reach him. He had the sense of a creature held in check by a harness that was long-worn. One of these days Anakin would break free . . . a thought that chilled Obi-Wan. But Obi-Wan chose to ignore those thoughts — out of friendship.

But he didn't want to tell Siri these things. What had she said, so many years ago? *We will be comrades.* Not best friends. She was not available for confidences. If he poured out his heart to her, where would he stop?

"I look back," he said, trying to find the words he wanted. "But I tell myself that the galaxy will be made safe with deeds, not regrets."

For some reason, his answer saddened her. He could see it in her eyes. "Yes," she said. "I hold onto duty. That's always saved me."

She jumped to her feet. In a flash, her mood had changed and she was back to the purposeful Jedi he knew best. "Speaking of which, we have twenty-four hours. We'd better get started."

CHAPTER 25

With access to Taly's records and a quick tour of the complex, the Jedi soon reached the conclusion that it was not going to be easy to solve Taly's problem.

"All of his employees are well paid," Anakin said. "They even own shares in the company. It would make no sense to throw it into disarray."

"Not only that, without Taly the company will cease to be profitable," Padmé said. "Every breakthrough and discovery has been his. There's no other inventor on his level on staff."

"I agree — it makes no sense for someone to try a takeover," Obi-Wan said.

"So is Taly just paranoid?" Siri asked. "He thinks his employees are out to get him, but they're loyal."

Obi-Wan shook his head. "Taly may be paranoid, but he's still sharp. I doubt he would invent a plot. And his inner office *is* under surveillance, according to our devices as well. So he didn't invent that. But I don't think someone is attempting a takeover."

"But you just said he didn't invent a plot," Padmé said.

"There is no takeover plot," Obi-Wan explained. "But there *is* a spy. Someone is out to steal the codebreaker. And I think the Separatists are behind it."

"Taly said there's been no unobserved communication since the codebreaker was developed," Siri pointed out. "We've gone over the comm monitoring system, and it's solid."

"That's because we're thinking like Jedi," Obi-Wan said to Siri. "How do the Separatists think? Someone very wise once said to me that they plant seeds. They're willing to wait years for results." Obi-Wan pointed to the holofiles that filled the air around them. "All the employee records look perfect because they are meant to."

"One of them is a mole," Siri said slowly, revolving to stare at all the files. "Someone planted here, years ago, because someone in the Separatists knew that Taly was a brilliant innovator, and that someday there would be something to steal."

"So they don't want the company," Padmé said. "They want the codebreaker. Only they don't know it's a codebreaker. Not yet."

"It has to be someone in the inner circle. Someone he trusts." Anakin said. "Helina Dow? Moro Y'Arano? Dellard Tranc, the head of security?"

"I don't know," Obi-Wan said. "We don't have to know. All we have to do is set the trap."

They had something going for them. Because of Taly's expert foiling of the office surveillance, the mole didn't know that Taly was aware of the bug. So they could plant information and set the trap.

They explained their plan to Taly, and he agreed. Then they gathered in his office.

"I'm glad we were able to come to terms," Taly said. "I think given the sensitive nature of the codebreaker, it would be best to get it out of the complex as soon as possible."

"We can leave tonight," Obi-Wan said. "Can you arrange for security to be lifted?"

"I will handle the security myself," Taly said. "I'll tell my staff after you leave that the codebreaker is gone. This deal is on a need-to-know basis, and nobody needs to know but me that the codebreaker is leaving until it's gone. Here."

Taly handed the codebreaker to Obi-Wan. It was a black metal box the size of a small suitcase. He slipped it into a carrying case.

"When you open it, a holographic file will appear that will explain the procedure for deployment," Taly said.

"We'll leave at nightfall," Siri said.

Night fell, and the Jedi and Padmé started on their walk to the hangar. Obi-Wan carried the codebreaker. He felt confident, or at least as confident as he ever allowed himself to feel. There was every chance that the mole would not realize that the Jedi were waiting. And three Jedi against one attacker would surely prevail.

Padmé, too, had grown quite handy with a blaster. Obi-Wan was always happy to have her on his side in a battle. Funny, Obi-Wan thought, how he had dismissed her when they'd first met. She had been so young, and posing as the queen's attendant, of course. He had seen her as someone he had to protect, not the fierce, determined ally she eventually proved herself to be. It was Qui-Gon who had seen her strength. Obi-Wan missed Qui-Gon with an acuteness that hadn't diminished in the long years since his death. There was still so much he wanted to learn from his former Master.

Anakin held up a hand. They could hear footsteps approaching. Helina Dow suddenly appeared around the corner. She smiled as she came forward.

"Taly told me to make sure you were escorted to your ship. He wanted you to know that security has been cleared for you."

Was this true? Obi-Wan doubted it. Still, he was surprised that Helina had turned out to be the spy. She had been with Taly from the beginning. She had built the company with him. It seemed strange that she would abandon all that she had gained.

"Here we are." Helina stopped in front of the entrance to the hangar. She bowed. "Have a safe journey."

Surprised, Obi-Wan half-turned to watch her go down the corridor. He raised an eyebrow at Anakin, who shrugged — then tensed as the Jedi walked through the hangar door.

They found themselves not in the hangar, but a small, windowless room. The door clanged shut behind them.

"She tricked us," Siri said. "We just walked through a holographic portal."

CHAPTER 26

Three lightsabers blazed to life. Within moments, they had cut a hole in the door. They rushed out into the corridor.

It was completely different. Instead of a set of double doors on one side and a corridor leading off to the right, there were doorways all the way down the corridor. Taly stood at the end of the corridor, smiling.

"What's going on?" Padmé shouted at him.

"It's a hologram," Anakin said, when Taly's image didn't answer.

"Helina Dow did this," Siri said. "There must be holograms all over this place. They use them for security."

"She wants to confuse us," Obi-Wan said. "But how does she expect to get the codebreaker?"

"Maybe she just wants to prevent us from leaving with it," Padmé said.

"Well, it doesn't matter. We know who the spy is. Let's tell Taly." Obi-Wan opened his comlink to contact Taly. There was no signal. "She must have blocked communication. This doesn't make sense. What is she hoping to accomplish?"

"Obi-Wan, maybe you should check the codebreaker," Padmé said.

A certain dread settled inside Obi-Wan as he flipped open the box. No holographic file appeared. He searched the database. No files were loaded.

"She switched it somehow," Siri said.

"Or Taly did," Anakin observed.

Siri and Obi-Wan exchanged a glance. They knew Taly hadn't switched the codebreaker. They believed in him, even after all these years. They remembered the boy who had run into a nest of pirates to save their lives. They knew that boy still lived in Taly.

"We've got to get to the hangar," Anakin said.

The low lighting made it harder to discern which of the doorways were holographic portals. It was impossible to navigate what they remembered as the route to the hangar. The Jedi charged down the hallway, Padmé trailing behind, letting them access the Force to discover which doors were holograms and which were real.

At last they found the doors to the hangar and charged through. Helina was ahead, racing to a cruiser, the codebreaker swinging with the motion of her run.

Obi-Wan and Anakin leaped at the same instant that Siri gave Helina a Force-push that sent her sprawling. The codebreaker slid away on the polished floor.

Obi-Wan and Anakin's boots thudded as they hit the ground near her head. She looked up at them, wide-eyed. "It's just business," she said. "Don't kill me."

"We're not going to kill you," Anakin said. "Who hired you?"

She shakily sat up, resting on her elbows. "Passel Argente hired me to get a job here five years ago. I was supposed to pass information along when I could to the Separatists. If something big came up, I was to steal it."

"Do they know about the codebreaker?"

"They know I'm bringing them something big. That's all. I can't send a communication, so I send out a code through one of Taly's business communications. It's to a supplier we've used for years, but Argente arranged to have someone there pass along the message to him."

Suddenly blaster fire lit the air and a smoke grenade exploded. Padmé dived to the floor, coughing. Anakin started toward her. Obi-Wan groped his way toward the codebreaker.

Someone else was here. Someone was firing, peppering the ground with blaster fire so fast it had to come from a repeating rifle.

The hangar bay doors were open, and the cool night air began to disperse the thick gray smoke. As it cleared, Obi-Wan saw the glint of a red-and-black starfighter. Someone was leaning out. He saw an arm sweep down and gather up the codebreaker.

He began to run, his eyes tearing from the smoke. The being wore an armorweave tunic and trousers as well as a full helmet with a breath mask, but Obi-Wan recognized him instantly.

It was Magus.

Taly suddenly ran into the hangar. Magus turned and saw him. Obi-Wan could not read his expression, but he sensed the satisfaction Magus felt as he aimed the repeating blaster even as he leaped back into his speeder.

Obi-Wan made a midair leap, his lightsaber swinging, as the intense fire ripped through the air. Behind him he felt Siri jump in front of Taly to protect him. Anakin blocked Padmé.

Magus turned and gave one more blast of fire. It hit Helina where she still lay stunned on the duracrete. She died instantly. Her usefulness to the Separatists was over, and she had become a liability.

Magus took off. Obi-Wan knew it was useless to go after him. By the time he got to a cruiser, Magus would be in the upper atmosphere.

He turned and walked toward Helina. He crouched next to her and allowed himself a moment to mourn the loss of a life.

"I can't believe it was Helina," Taly said, his voice hollow.

"Magus got the codebreaker," Siri said.

Taly shook his head. "Helina only thought she had it. We made two prototypes. She took one, but I put a bug in it. I'm the only one who knows where the real one is."

"Magus is no doubt taking it to the Separatists," Siri said.

"We have to get the codebreaker to the Republic

before the Separatists know the one they have is a fake," Obi-Wan said. "We have to monitor their broadcasts."

"Bring it to us," Padmé told Taly, sounding like the queen she had once been.

"I have it," Taly said, opening his tunic to reveal the codebreaker strapped across his chest. "And I'm coming with you. If Magus is after me again, I want your personal guarantee for my safety for the duration of the Clone Wars. That's a condition of your purchase of the code-breaker."

Padmé gave him a cool glance. "You never stop nego-tiating, do you?"

"I just want what I want."

"This is your last condition," she told him. "And you had better guarantee that this box is the real codebreaker."

Taly grinned, and the boy Obi-Wan had known was back. "It is."

CHAPTER 27

They blasted off for the Azure Spaceport. The finest tech experts in the Republic army were already there, waiting to receive the codebreaking device.

Obi-Wan spoke to Anakin. "I suggest you get some rest on the journey. And Padmé looks exhausted. If you could persuade her that she needs rest, it would do her good."

Anakin's gaze was opaque.

I so rarely know what he is thinking anymore, Obi-Wan thought.

"Yes, Master," Anakin said.

He is still obedient, but it is as though he makes an effort to be so.

Obi-Wan watched as Anakin went over to speak quietly to Padmé. She nodded, and the two of them left the cockpit.

That left Siri and Taly and Obi-Wan. Siri kept her eyes on the instruments, even though Obi-Wan had plotted the course and there wasn't much for her to do. It all felt so familiar, the three of them in a cockpit, heading away from danger and most likely into more of it.

"Tell me something, Taly," Obi-Wan said, spinning around in his chair to face him. "Passel Argente placed Helina Dow in your employ. She bided her time, but Argente always meant to destroy you. Why are you still protecting him?"

"Protecting him?"

"He hired those bounty hunters and you never told the Senate."

"It was my last bargaining chip."

"But he hired Magus, and Magus killed your parents."

"Magus did that for revenge. I didn't blame Argente for their deaths. I blame Magus." Taly's face grew hard.

"So why didn't you tell?"

"I knew I would have to start over," Taly said. "I knew I needed a patron. I waited until I was older, and then I approached him when I was ready to take back my name and start my company. Who do you think gave me my first business loan?"

Obi-Wan shook his head ruefully. Qui-Gon had been right. Taly had known all along, and he had used that information. It must have taken an enormous amount of nerve to contact Passel Argente and demand hush money.

"I used Argente, but I never trusted him. He ended up coming at me in a way I didn't expect. But if I went to the Senate today and told some committee about a twenty-year-old plot, they'd laugh me out of the chambers. They have enough problems. Everything has changed, hasn't it? My best revenge on Argente now is to help you win the Clone Wars."

"Well, that's one thing we should be grateful for, at least," Siri said. She seemed more amused than irritated by Taly.

Taly approached her. "I have something for you." He held out his hand. Siri's old warming crystal lay in his palm, the cool deep blue of the crystal glowing slightly.

She took it wonderingly. "But how —"

"I went back to Settlement Five and bought it back from the same vendor you sold it to," he said. "I tracked him down. I always wanted to give it to you someday."

"Thank you, Taly," Siri said. She closed her fingers over it. A flush of pleasure lit her face.

"You think I don't remember," he said to both of them. "I remember how you fought for me. I remember everything."

He walked out of the cockpit. Obi-Wan gave a quick glance at Siri.

And you, Siri — do you remember everything?

She was keeping her face from him. They had buried this for so long. But how could they keep forgetting, when the reminders were so real?

"I promised you once never to remind you," Obi-Wan said.

"It's not you who is reminding me, though, is it?" A smile touched Siri's lips. "So much time has passed."

"And so little."

"And we've changed so much."

"Yes. You're more beautiful." The words left Obi-Wan before he could stop them. "And smarter, and stronger."

"And you," Siri said, "you've grown sadder."

"You can see that?"

"Forgive me if I still think I know you better than anybody else."

"You do."

"I don't regret our decision," Siri said. "I wouldn't want to go back and change it. Would you?"

"No," Obi-Wan said. "It was the right one. But . . ."

"Yes," Siri said. "It doesn't prevent you from regrets, does it? Regrets you can live with. It took me awhile, but I realized that Yoda and Qui-Gon were right. I would have regretted leaving the Jedi Order every day of my life. And that is not a life I would want to live. I've lived the life I wanted to live."

"I'm glad." Obi-Wan felt the same. But was it that simple for him? He wasn't sure. Somehow, on this trip, he was fully understanding, for the first time, how many regrets he did have. And secrets.

"What I regret," he said, "was not so much the decision we made, but what happened to us afterward. When we made the decision to part, it made our friendship become something else. Something that couldn't be quite as close as it should have been."

"Comrades, not best friends," Siri said.

He nodded. His other deep friendships — with Garen

and Bant — were different. With them, he felt no barriers. With Siri, there was always a barrier. He did not think of it or speak of it, but it was always there. He wished it hadn't been. In some way he couldn't quite define, he felt like he had lost her twice.

"Well, it's not too late, is it?" Siri asked. "It took us almost twenty years to talk to each other about the past. Maybe now we can be the friends we were meant to be. I would like that. I'm tired of pushing away the past."

"Best friends, then."

Siri smiled, and the years fell away. Obi-Wan felt it then, the pain in his heart he had put away with his memories. It was as vivid as Siri's grin.

"Best friends," she agreed.

CHAPTER 28

"You're going to tell me to live in the present moment," Padmé said to Anakin. "But I can't help it. We have the codebreaker. We have a chance now to end it all, a real chance."

They were in her stateroom, the one they had insisted on giving Padmé, the largest and most comfortable. She of course had tried to refuse. She could sleep in the cargo hold, or in a chair, she didn't care. They knew this was true, but something about Padmé made beings want to give to her.

He wanted to give her everything, but of course, she would not want it. Navigating his marriage with Padmé was like stumbling through a dark room sometimes, Anakin thought. He had believed on their wedding day that love would see them through any difficulty. What they felt was so huge that it would crash through every barrier.

He still believed that with all his heart. But he had not imagined, on the day of his wedding, that some of those barriers would lie within his wife herself. He did not think that he wouldn't be able to talk her out of putting herself in danger. He had secretly hoped that, in time, she would resign her Senate seat. As the wars went on, she would see how ridiculous it was to try to talk planets out of something that would bring them more power or more wealth.

Now he saw how naïve he'd been. She would never quit the Senate. She would keep talking about justice with the last breath in her body. She believed that words mattered.

He accepted that. He was even proud of her reputation as a sharp-tongued orator. In the Senate, held together somehow by the strength of Palpatine, she had made enemies. He feared for her. It was a nameless dread that sometimes could clutch him by the throat and drive the air from his lungs.

"We're not at Azure yet," he said. "And it won't be long before the Separatists come after us. Did you see how Magus targeted Taly? Now they know that Taly has contacted us, and that means he cannot be allowed to live. If he throws his knowledge on the side of the Republic, they'll do anything to stop him. His life is not safe until the Clone Wars are over."

"I didn't think of that," Padmé said. "Of course that is true."

"The Jedi must remain on Azure to ensure that the Republic experts can deploy the codebreaker. Then we must accompany the experts to another safe location. At least in the beginning, we're going to have to keep moving. That's why you must return immediately to Coruscant with Taly."

Her expression turned flinty. "That sounds like another order."

"No. It is a necessary step to protect you and Taly, and you know it. And it is a request," he said, softening his voice. He was relieved when he saw her slowly nod.

"All right."

"Padmé." He reached out for her hand. He needed the reassurance he felt when he touched her. "Your job lies in the Senate. My job lies is in the field. Until these wars are over, that is the way it must be."

"I hate these separations."

"No more than I."

"We chose this life," she said. "But it's so hard to live it."

"It's worth it, to know that you're mine. But if anything happened to you, I don't know how I could survive it. I can't . . . I can't lose you."

"I feel the same."

She stood, her cool fingers sliding out from between his. She began to pace. "But the secrecy is tearing me apart. I'm always afraid I'll betray us with a look or a word. Sometimes I wonder . . ."

"What?" he asked. If she hadn't been so agitated, she would have recognized the tone in his voice, a warning.

She whirled to face him. "Did we do the right thing? Not in loving each other — we couldn't help that — but in marrying? I've put a wedge between you and the Jedi."

"No, you haven't."

"But your first loyalty is to me," Padmé said. "That makes your path confused. I know enough about the Jedi to know how wrong that is."

"It is *they* who are wrong." Anakin insisted. "I am strong enough to do both, and they can't see it."

The comm unit crackled, and they sprang apart instinctively. They heard Obi-Wan's voice. "Anakin, are you there? Come to the cockpit immediately."

They hurried down the corridor into the cockpit. Taly was standing with the codebreaker. There was a mixture of awe and trepidation on Obi-Wan's face.

"It works," Obi-Wan said. "We've been listening to coded Separatist communications. It really works."

"There's too much space interference here," Taly said. "We have to get to the spaceport. Clearing devices can be used with it But we were able to hear something."

"What did you hear?" Anakin asked.

"They are moving ships and troops," Obi-Wan said. "A massive battle is planned. But we can't seem to pinpoint the location. Originally, it seemed to be planned for Nativum, which we suspected. But that changed to a new target recently."

"If we find out in time, we could score a great victory," Padmé said.

Obi-Wan nodded. "We could destroy most of their fleet."

Padmé gripped the console. "If General Grievous is with it, we could win the war," she said.

CHAPTER **29**

Azure was a tiny planet with no strategic importance. It was a blue dot in a vast expanse of space. It stood alone, not part of a system, and had no satellites. It boasted a spaceport that took up a good portion of its land. A convenient waystation for those traveling through the Mid-Rim, but not a draw in itself. It had no industry, no minerals, and no great wealth.

In other words, it had no reason to exist in the minds of the Separatists, and made a perfect secret base for the Republic, one of many in the galaxy.

They landed without incident. It seemed impossible that they had come so far, had made the journey without trouble. The crucial piece of equipment that could turn the tide of the war was now in Republic hands.

Taly handed it over to the tech experts with regret on his face. "It is my greatest invention," he said. "Now I must lead the life of a fugitive."

The cluster of tech experts hurriedly transported the codebreaker off to the command post. They were followed closely by General Solomahal. Recently promoted to the post, the Lutrillian could hardly contain his satisfaction at having the codebreaker arrive at his base. He had assured the Jedi that the name of Azure would live on in the chronicles of the war.

"This is the day the war will be won," he said, the large furrows in his head deepening.

Anakin didn't approve of such talk. The war had not been won yet. Even if they found out where the Separatist fleet was heading, it remained to be seen whether they could get enough Republic ships organized for a surprise attack.

Still, it was hard to concentrate on the matters at hand when Padmé was leaving. He had tried to contrive a way to say good-bye to her alone, but it would attract too much suspicion. They would have to bid farewell to each other in public. He hated that. She told him with her eyes that she hated it, too.

"Good-bye, Senator Amidala," Obi-Wan said, bowing. "Have a safe journey, and may the Force be with you."

He stood there, not moving, waiting for Anakin to say good-bye. Anakin swallowed his resentment. It wasn't his Master's fault that he did not give him privacy.

Anakin bowed. When he lifted his head, he told her with his gaze how much he would miss her. "Safe journey, Senator. I'm sure we'll meet again soon."

"I'm sure we shall." *Soon,* she mouthed to him.

"Taly, you have done a great service to the galaxy," Obi-Wan said.

"We are grateful," Siri said.

"I hope the war ends quickly," Taly said. "Even though it's good for business."

His eyes twinkled when he said it. Was he really as cynical as he appeared? Anakin didn't think so.

Under the cover of her robes, Padmé placed her hand in Anakin's, squeezed it for a moment, then dropped it. The touch was so quick that he barely had time to register it.

She had mentioned regrets. He had never had a chance to ask her what she meant. Now she was going and he didn't know when he'd see her again.

Padmé walked up the ramp of the cruiser. General Solomahal could not spare a pilot so Padmé would guide the ship to Coruscant, with a few clone troopers accompanying her for protection. She sat close to the windscreen so that she could see Anakin. She didn't lift a hand or smile but she kept her gaze on his as she fired the engines. Then the silver ship lifted and streaked into the sky.

Anakin kept his eyes on it. Was this his fate, he wondered, to know that something was his, but yet never be able to truly possess it?

He heard the stamp of boots behind him, but he didn't turn. He wanted to watch the silver ship.

"We have a problem," General Solomahal's voice boomed out.

Anakin turned reluctantly.

"There was a tracer imbedded in the codebreaker," General Solomahal said.

"Helina Dow," Siri said. "She must have put them in both prototypes."

"So the Separtists might know it's here on Azure," Obi-Wan said.

"I think that's a fair assumption," General Solomahal said. "The reason you could not pinpoint the site of the Separatist attack was because there was not yet a target. Not then. They were waiting to see where the codebreaker would end up." The General paused. "The target is here. The Separatist fleet is heading to Azure spaceport."

CHAPTER 30

The Jedi rushed to the command center. Countermeasures had already been ordered. Every available ship in the Republic fleet was streaming toward Azure.

But they were hours away.

"How many battle cruisers do you have in the spaceport?" Anakin asked the general.

"Not enough," he said grimly. "A small fleet. Here." He called up the list on the datascreen. Anakin leaned over to study the specifications.

"Let's divide the fleet into two divisions," Anakin decided crisply. "Hold off the second for spaceport defense. I'll lead the first to try to draw off some of the Separatist fleet. Our strongest chance is to keep them busy until the bulk of the Republic ships arrive. I'll need your best pilots."

The general blinked his heavy-lidded eyes at Anakin, as if he needed time to process that a commander was giving orders to the general in charge. Luckily, General Solomahal was a practical sort, a soldier who did not care where the best tactical ideas came from, as long as they came.

"Lieutenant Banno," General Solomahal said, turning

to a tall Bothan at his side. "Take Jedi Commander Skywalker to the fleet. He'll be in charge."

The lieutenant nodded. Anakin started away, but Obi-Wan put a hand on his arm. "Anakin, take care. May the Force be with you."

Anakin nodded, but Obi-Wan could see that his mind was already moving on to the battle ahead. They could have no better air commander than Anakin for this battle.

The lieutenant and Anakin hurried off. Obi-Wan and Siri turned to the large, circular monitor in the center of the command room. The Separatist fleet was close enough now to be tracked.

Obi-Wan could see instantly by the size of the fleet that the spaceport was extremely vulnerable. Siri frowned at the monitor.

"Here," she said, grabbing a laser pointer. "And here. That's where they are vulnerable. If Anakin can get to the rear —"

Obi-Wan nodded. "We don't have to defeat them. We just have to slow them down."

"They don't know that we have the codebreaker working, so it's possible they're expecting to launch a surprise attack," Siri said. "That could be an advantage for us. Do you see this small cloud nebula? If Anakin could get his ships to lurk there until the last possible second, when the fleet has already passed him . . ."

Obi-Wan was already pushing the comm button. He

quickly gave Anakin the coordinates of the nebula. "Do you see it?"

"I've got it. There's quite a bit of atmospheric disturbance within it," Anakin said. "I might lose communication capability temporarily."

"We'll have to risk it. Then if you could manage to sneak down the side flank to the rear — that's where the big gunners are."

"Got it."

They watched as the blip that was Anakin's ship peel off, followed by the rest of the small fleet.

Obi-Wan turned to General Solomahal. "You'll have to time the countermeasure artillery attack to when Anakin attacks the rear. There will be confusion then. I'd try to hit the lead ship."

He nodded. His face was grim. "We will do our best, Commander."

"They are approaching the outer atmosphere of Azure airspace," Siri said. "There are some civilian ships heading into deep space . . ." Suddenly one blip flared and disappeared. "They're firing on civilian ships!"

A sinking feeling hit Obi-Wan. "Where are Padmé and Taly? Are they out of range?"

Siri went pale. "They're on the fleet's right flank."

Obi-Wan reached for his comlink, but suddenly Padmé's voice filled the air. "Come in, General. They're firing on us. . . . We can't hold the ship. . . ."

"Evacuate!" Obi-Wan shouted at her.

"Anakin!" Padmé shouted.

The blip that was Padmé's ship flared and disappeared.

"It's gone," Siri said. "Padmé's gone."

CHAPTER 31

"No," Obi-Wan said. "They got to an escape pod. Look." He pointed to the monitor. A tiny pulse was moving. It could have been space debris, but Obi-Wan knew it was Padmé. He could feel it.

"She's going to land outside the spaceport. We have to help them," Siri said.

"There are starfighters fueled and waiting in the hangar," the general said. "We still have the codebreaker working on communications. Keep your comm open and I'll feed you information."

They ran to the hangar and leaped into the two starfighters at the head of the line. Nearby pilots were rushing to their ships. Anakin had burst out of the nebula and hit the fleet in the rear with his small squadron. The battle had begun.

Obi-Wan and Siri took off, flying in formation.

"I've received a distress call from the planet's surface," General Solomahal said, giving them the coordinates. "It's out where the survival systems for the planet are based — the water conduits, the fuel tanks, the fusion generators. Watch your flank — the fleet is planning to turn at eighty degrees."

Obi-Wan and Siri executed a diving turn to avoid the fleet. Obi-Wan could hear the chatter of the pilots on the comm. Anakin was flying brilliantly, taking chances that the pilots could not quite believe and inspiring them to try similar feats.

By the end of the Clone Wars, he'll be a legend, Obi-Wan thought.

The air around the ship suddenly lit up. Obi-Wan felt the thud of cannonfire.

"On your left!" Siri shouted.

He turned and went into a screaming dive. Siri followed.

"Two starfighters have been ordered to break off and follow you," General Solomahal barked. "They are ordered to shoot you down." He quickly told Obi-Wan and Siri the angle of attack.

They were able to turn at the last minute and surprise their attackers. Laser cannonfire boomed, and the ships went into spiraling, smoking ruin.

Obi-Wan and Siri peeled off and continued toward their goal. From this angle, they were far enough away to get a clear look at the battle.

His heart sank. He believed in Anakin. He believed in the strength and will of the Republic pilots. But he knew the exact time it would take for the rest of the Republic fleet to arrive. The battle was already lost.

His heart heavy, he contacted General Solomahal.

"General, I suggest you give the codebreaker to your best pilot and get it off the spaceport now. We have to risk it. We can't have the codebreaker fall into Separatist hands."

"Are you insane, General Kenobi?" The general's voice boomed out. "That's our only hedge against disaster!"

"I agree with Commander Kenobi," Siri said. "It's vital that the codebreaker remain safe. We can see clearly from up here. Ultimately, we cannot win this battle. I also suggest that you stand by to evacuate the base. We need to save as many Republic soldiers and ships as we can."

"It's a little early for surrender."

"I agree. There are still blows that can be struck. But it's inevitable," Obi-Wan said. "We need to cut our losses."

"You are too cautious, Commander Kenobi. I think we can win this."

"Commander, we can see things better up here," Siri said.

"I have a monitor here, too, Commander Tachi. And I don't have time for this argument. Save your Senator and your scientist and come back to fight."

Cannonfire blasted, and the controls shook in Obi-Wan's hands. He and Siri had blundered into the center of a battle between Republic starships and an attack ship they were peppering with fire and trying to disable. Obi-Wan saw cannonfire rip into his hull. Smoke poured from Siri's fighter. Quickly, they zoomed up and around the battle. When they were through the worst of the fire, they returned to their course and dived down to the planet's surface.

Obi-Wan heard his comm unit crackling. He must have sustained some damage to the circuitry when the ship was hit.

They saw the escape pod resting in an industrial area. Padmé had guided it to a safe landing between gigantic fuel tanks. Obi-Wan let out a low whistle as he landed gingerly next to her. It must have taken nerves of steel to navigate between those tanks. Escape pods weren't known for their maneuverability.

Siri landed close by and they hurried over to Padmé, who was holding a blaster rifle casually at her side. Her clone trooper escort must have landed elsewhere, but the pod had had enough room for Taly to join her.

"Happy to see you," she said, though her face betrayed her. She was disappointed, too. She'd been hoping for something, Obi-Wan thought. The answer sprang instantly to mind. *Anakin.*

"Anakin is in command of the air battle at the moment," he told her.

She smiled briefly. "How close is the Republic fleet?"

"Still hours away," Siri said.

"Even a codebreaker can't save this battle, can it?" Taly guessed shrewdly.

Obi-Wan decided not to answer the question. No matter what his doubts, he wouldn't want to voice them except to the commanding general.

But Padmé, too, was too shrewd not to see. She glanced up at the sky. "We should get the codebreaker off planet."

"Let's escort you and Taly to safety first," Siri said. "I think one of us should pilot you out of here."

"We can return to the command post," Padmé suggested.

Obi-Wan shook his head. "Not safe. We'll have to get you through enemy lines and to the nearest safe port." But which of them would do it? He looked over at Siri. They both wanted to stay to fight the battle, but she knew that it would be harder for him to leave his Padawan.

He felt the dark side surge then, a warning so clear he heard it like a shout. A starfighter was streaking toward them. Obi-Wan recognized the red-and-silver starfighter of Magus. He was surrounded by five droid tri-fighters.

"Take cover!" Obi-Wan yelled.

The laser cannons tore up the ground as they scattered.

"We can't hide behind fuel tanks," Siri said. "That's madness. We'll get blown up."

Magus came in for another assault. The fire hit the fuel tank, and it exploded in a whoosh that sent them flying through the air. The air was like a flaming wall that hit Obi-Wan like an obstacle. He felt himself falling, and it was like falling through pure fire.

They landed, bruised and shaken, but unhurt. Magus and the tri-fighters zoomed out and turned, heading for another strike.

"I think it's time we got out of here," Obi-Wan said.

CHAPTER 32

Siri and Padmé were closest to Siri's ship. They began to run through the thick black smoke and burning fires. Obi-Wan grabbed Taly and hustled him toward his own ship.

This time Magus bypassed Siri and Padmé, coming straight for Taly.

Obi-Wan noticed that a worker had left his servotool kit close by. He reached out a hand — a fusioncutter flew through the air toward him. It was a large one with a big tank, built for special jobs. He grabbed it and timed his response. At the last possible second, he activated the fusioncutter and flung it directly into the spilled fuel. The fuel ignited and the flame shot up just as Magus dived to strafe them again.

Magus had to climb to avoid the fire, and the smoke was good cover. Obi-Wan and Taly leaped into the ARC 170 starfighter and took off after Siri.

"He's after you," Obi-Wan said.

"No kidding," Taly answered.

Siri flew closer and made a gesture, her hand at her throat. Obi-Wan did the same.

"What does that mean?"

"Our comm units are out," Obi-Wan said. "They were damaged. We're on our own."

"More good news."

Siri signaled. Obi-Wan nodded.

"You two speak the same language without even talking," Taly said. "Not much has changed. What's the plan?"

"We're going to try to get the two of you out of harm's way, then return for the end of the battle," Obi-Wan said.

"The end of the battle? Considering that you're going to lose, that doesn't sound like such a wise idea."

"I can't leave my Padawan. Hang on."

They zoomed upward. But Magus was on their tail with his five fighters, keeping up a steady barrage of firepower. The starship shook. Siri dived under Magus and shot, clipping him just a fraction. He zoomed off.

They played cat-and-mouse games. Every time they got ahead, he found them. Siri destroyed one of the tri-fighters, and Obi-Wan scored a direct hit on another. Then, working in tandem, they squeezed two between them and blasted them into space debris.

Magus must have contacted the Separatist fleet for help, for two large attack missiles suddenly peeled off from the battle above and began to descend.

"This doesn't look good," Taly said.

No. It wasn't good.

Obi-Wan raced his craft toward Siri. When he was in her sightline, he indicated with his chin what he thought they should do. She nodded. He felt the connection surge between them. This was more than the Force. It was part of the Force, but it was part of them, part of the understanding that flashed between them so freely now. All barriers down, they had locked onto each other's every thought now.

They were over the deep trenches of the electrical conduits, where power flowed from the two gigantic fusion furnaces that supplied the energy to the spaceport. Siri dipped into the trench, and Obi-Wan followed. At least they were in a place where the large attack missiles could not follow. And if they were lucky, they could escape Magus in the maze.

The battle was lost. Anakin could see that. As much as he believed in his abilities, as much as he believed in the pilots around him, he could see that they were meeting an overwhelming force, and according to General Solomahal, Republic reenforcements were still an hour away.

At first he'd felt hopeful. The information the general was able to give the pilots gave them an edge they were able to exploit. They had taken down one starfighter after another and had managed to cripple a landing ship. But they could not fight this huge fleet.

He had lost track of Obi-Wan and Siri. But at least Padmé was safe.

". . . status report," came over the comm. "Report in, Leader One."

His comm unit sounded fuzzy. Another thing going wrong. "Five more starfighters down, "Anakin said. "I'm trying to slow down the second landing ship. None of our ships lost on this end."

"Two of our defense starfighters down, plus the three civilian ships and the Republic cruiser . . ."

The interference made the words come in and out. "What?" Anakin barked. "What Republic cruiser?"

"Senator Amidala . . . Under fire . . . Distress . . ."

"Repeat," Anakin said desperately. "Repeat. Survivors?"

"No survivors . . ."

Anakin felt the galaxy collapse. He could not see or think or feel.

"Jedi went in search . . . Possible . . . escape pod sighting . . ."

Anakin went into a dive that nearly plastered him to the ceiling. He would find her. She would be alive. She had to be.

Obi-Wan wished that Anakin were flying this ship. He needed Anakin's nerves, his split-second timing, his instinctive knowledge of exactly how far to push a craft.

The attack ships hovered overhead. The last of the droid tri-fighters had crashed into a wall and flamed out. But Magus was on their tails, keeping up steady fire. The trench was narrow, and opened wider and narrowed again.

Huge pipes and conduits presented barriers that had to be snaked around or dived under.

Up ahead, Siri suddenly slowed her speed. He shot ahead but she didn't follow. She flew up, almost to the edge of the trench.

Siri, what are you doing? Whatever it is, Obi-Wan thought with a sudden, sharp pain, *don't do it!*

"Siri, don't do it," Padmé said. "There's still a chance —"

"*This* is our chance. Can you hold it steady?"

Padmé nodded.

"When I tell you to cut back, cut back."

"You'll fall —"

Siri grinned. "No, I won't. I'll jump."

"No —"

But Siri was already opening the hatch and climbing out. This was a model that had room for an astromech droid, if the pilot wanted. The space was empty. She felt the wind whip through her hair. She saw Obi-Wan's ship in the near distance. No doubt he was wondering what she was up to.

She knew this was crazy, but it just might work.

Magus dove through the last of a series of pipes. She could see the exact moment when he realized she'd cut her speed. He cut his, too, to avoid running into her. He didn't want to get ahead of her. That would make him vulnerable to her fire.

"Cut your speed!" Siri yelled, and she felt the ship slow and come close to stopping.

Magus shot underneath and slowed again, not wanting to get ahead of the Jedi ship. Summoning the Force, Siri leaped.

The starfighters had slowed, but they were still moving. Jumping from one to another was not easy. To say the least. Siri used the Force to slow her perception of time. She had never felt so in tune with it. She felt her body turning, but it was turning just as she wanted it to, not propelled by the speed of her descent or the turbulent air, but moving exactly so.

She hit the ship. Her knees buckled and her hands slapped against the top of the hull. The fall had knocked the wind out of her and for a moment all she could do was try to hold on. She clamped a cable from her belt to the ship.

He still didn't know she was there. She was light enough and he was moving fast enough, firing at Padmé now, who had immediately increased speed. He did not hear or feel her.

Time to let him know he had an extra passenger.

She activated her lightsaber and began to cut through the top of the starfighter.

It lurched violently to the left.

Siri grimaced as she held on with one hand.

Magus knew she was here.

*   *   *

Obi-Wan realized too late that this trench was a dead end. He should have taken one of the branches, but he was distracted at the sight of Siri on top of a starfighter. She had to be crazy. What she was doing was impossible. But she was doing it.

He would have to pull up in a few short minutes. The attack cruisers were waiting to blow him out of the sky. He would have to double back somehow. There was barely enough room to maneuver, let alone turn around.

Behind him, Magus was flying erratically, zooming from one edge of the trench to the other, trying to knock Siri off. Obi-Wan couldn't believe how she was managing to continue to cut through the ship's shell as she was slammed repeatedly against the metal.

He had to do something.

"Any ideas?" Taly asked.

"Yes. Hang on," Obi-Wan said as he flipped the ship upside down.

It was a maneuver he'd seen Anakin do, fly backward and upside down. *Though I wouldn't recommend it,* Anakin had said with a grin.

Obi-Wan headed straight for Magus. Padmé zoomed out of his way, then up out of the trench for a moment. Evading fire, she managed to zoom past Magus and start back along the trench, marking time. *Good move, Padmé.*

Obi-Wan did some quick calculations. His fingers flew on the weapons-system control board. It was hard to fly at the same time.

"What are you doing?" Taly asked.

"Disarming a concussion missile by half."

"Let me do it." Taly worked over the keyboard, fingers flying. "Done."

Obi-Wan slowed his speed. He didn't want to get too close — he had to be far enough away, past the top end of the missile's range, so that he didn't severely damage the ship. All he needed was shock waves. That, and Siri's command of the Force to know what was coming before Magus did.

He fired. The concussion missile flew and exploded.

The shock wave jolted Siri, but she recovered quickly.

Magus went flying. Obi-Wan saw him bounce out of the seat. At that instant, Siri dropped through the hole she had created.

The ship was careening crazily now. Siri was fighting for control. Obi-Wan reversed again. He thought he saw a dark shape move across the cockpit.

"They're fighting," Taly said.

The ship listed to one side. It spun out of control and clipped a gigantic pipe. Smoke began to pour out of the exhausts.

"The hydraulics are failing," Taly said anxiously.

Obi-Wan began to follow the route of the dying ship. He pushed the engines, but he watched in horror as the ship crashed into the trench. Sparks as big as fireballs flew in the air as it bounced against one wall, then another, then smashed into the side and stopped. Something flew out of the hole on the top, bounced and lay still. Magus.

Obi-Wan screamed down to the trench bottom. He activated the cockpit cover and leaped out. Magus was unmoving but he wasn't dead. Obi-Wan scrambled on top of the cruiser and dropped inside.

Was it now, or was it twenty years ago?

She lay on the floor of the cockpit in a crashed ship. Her blond head was pillowed in her arms.

He landed on his knees by her side.

He touched her hair. He could not bear to touch the pulse on her neck. He could not bear not to feel life there.

"Siri."

"Blasterfire." She groaned as she turned slightly so she could look up at him. "Magus."

Obi-Wan glanced out of the cockpit window where Padmé now stood, holding the rifle at the unconscious Magus. She was taking no chances. Taly stood next to her, a blaster in his hand, also pointed at Magus. Obi-Wan could see something working in Taly's face, a temptation to fire. He had, at his feet, the being who had killed his parents.

Above, in the sky, he saw Anakin diving around the attack cruisers, pummeling them with fire.

"Padmé has him covered. We're safe for the moment."

"Everything is so gray."

"That was such a risky move," Obi-Wan said.

"It worked, didn't it?"

His relief at her sharp tone was erased when she winced, and he saw she was in great pain.

"I'll get the bacta . . ."

"Don't leave me." Siri's hand dropped on his. "I wanted to say —"

"Siri, I must get the med kit —"

"For star's sake, Obi-Wan, I'm dying. Do you have to interrupt me now?"

Tears sprang to his eyes. "You're not dying."

Her fingers plucked at her belt. "I can't . . . Get it for me."

Get what? he almost asked, but then he knew. He slipped her crystal out of her belt and pressed it into her hand.

"No . . . yours." She let it fall into his palm. "Now I will never leave you."

"You will never leave me," he repeated.

She touched his cheek, and her hand fell. "Don't worry so much," she said.

Her eyes closed, and she was gone.

He lay his head on the cockpit floor and held her hand. He did not know, at that moment, what living was for, if he had to carry this pain.

Anakin had been out of his mind with the frenzy to find her. He had attacked the ships again and again, determined to slip through.

When he saw that a ship had crashed, he had thought Padmé was dead, and his heart had become a fist.

Revenge was all he wanted.

And then as he swooped down he had seen her, blaster rifle in her hand, her face turned up toward him.

He held her to him only seconds later.

"I'm afraid for Siri," she whispered.

Obi-Wan climbed out of the ruined ship. He came toward them. Something in his face, his walk was different.

"She has joined the Force." He spoke the words to them, but he was looking down at Magus. The bounty hunter was beginning to stir. Taly gripped the blaster tighter. Anakin saw strain and anguish in his face.

He wants to shoot, Anakin thought.

For the first time since he'd known Obi-Wan Kenobi, Anakin was afraid for his Master. He saw the way he looked at Magus. His eyes were dead, as if now there was nothing at his feet, not a living being, just clothes and hair and skin.

Obi-Wan activated his lightsaber.

Padmé looked at Anakin, her eyes wide. *Say something,* her face pleaded. *Stop him.*

Anakin recognized that there was something here he could not stop.

Taly's breath caught. He did not take his eyes off Obi-Wan.

Obi-Wan crouched down and held the glowing

lightsaber to Magus's neck. He locked eyes with Magus. Anakin saw the flare of fear in the bounty hunter's eyes.

"You kill without thought or feeling," Obi-Wan said. "But I am not you."

He stood.

"Take him aboard," Obi-Wan said. "He is now a prisoner of war."

CHAPTER 33

The codebreaker was lost in the Battle of Azure Space-port. The fusion furnace blew, an explosion that came close to leveling the spaceport itself. The smoke that rose served as cover for the evacuation of Republic ships. General Solomahal was captured with the codebreaker as he attempted to escape with it. He blew it up instead of handing it over. Two days later, he managed to escape and was given another command.

The Separatist forces bombed Taly's laboratory. All his notes and documents were lost. It could take him years to reinvent what he had discovered . . . if he could reproduce it at all. In the meantime, he was taken in secrecy and transported to a Republic outpost.

On Coruscant, Anakin and Padmé met before dawn in her apartment on her veranda. It was their favorite time to meet, under cover of darkness, but with the beginnings of morning freshness in the air. Even in the darkest of times, it made them feel hopeful.

"I am being sent away again," he told her. "Obi-Wan and I leave this morning."

"There is a vote I must attend this morning," Padmé said. "So we must say good-bye here."

"A vote is so important?"

"They are all important now. Senator Organa needs my support."

Anakin made an impatient gesture, but he did not want to fight. He was still struck with the horror of almost losing her. But he did not understand these Senate votes, useless during a time of war when only battles won mattered.

"I will wait for you to return," Padmé said. "I will wait as long as I must."

Anakin's eyes lifted to the Jedi Temple. What did they know, Yoda and Obi-Wan and Mace, of this? Of this moment of agony, being torn from his wife. He fought for them and alongside them, but they no longer had his heart. They no longer understood him.

He had thought for a moment on Azure that Obi-Wan had loved Siri. He thought he'd seen it in his Master's eyes after she had died. But Obi-Wan had stood over the man who had killed her and spared him. If he had loved Siri, could he have done that? Of course, it was what a Jedi should do. But the way Obi-Wan had spoken had been so measured. With a temperament like that, it was impossible to love, Anakin was sure.

With Padmé, he had passion, and he was whole. The stars began to disappear above, and a thin line of orange indicated the sun was beginning to rise. They would lose the cover of darkness. They would once again be Jedi and Senator.

— He would once again be split in two.

For several nights now, Obi-Wan had not been able to sleep. He lay on his sleep couch. He closed his eyes. He hoped to dream. He could not.

So he walked. Through the Temple, the glow lights a faint blue. He did not seek the places that reminded him of Siri. He couldn't do that, not yet.

Oddly, he thought of Qui-Gon on these walks. He remembered, as he had not remembered in years, how he had known that Qui-Gon had walked the Temple halls at night. He had taken him *sapir* tea, he remembered. He had tried to comfort him, even though he knew there was no comfort for him.

If Anakin knew of his grief, he didn't mention it. He, too, had risen early — Obi-Wan had seen him heading toward the exit. Anakin had always been restless, had always needed to escape the Temple to think. Something was between him and Padmé. Obi-Wan would not ask. In some ways, he envied it. Let Anakin make his own decisions.

He found it extraordinary that at the time of this grief, when he had lost Siri forever, he did not question that their parting twenty years ago had been the right thing. He saw that clearly now, more clearly than he had ever seen it. Love was different from possession. He had loved her. That was enough.

. . . *I live with the heartbreak of losing her. But I am living, Obi-Wan. I am continuing to walk the Jedi path.*

This was what he had learned — the Jedi had kept him from her. But the Jedi had taught him how to live with losing her.

Obi-Wan stood by the window. The blues and grays outside were changing, warming to pink. Orange streaks lit the sky. The space lanes were beginning to fill up with flashes of silver. Another day. Another mission.

He was ready. He had learned something else, something important. Once he'd thought he had to lock away memories of love. Now he was no longer afraid of them. He could live with them. He could breathe in his sadness and remember his joy.

At last he had learned the secret that Qui-Gon had always tried to teach him. It had taken him years of loss to learn it. It had taken a death that had sent him to his knees. But he had finally learned it. He had learned to live with an open heart.